"Lila and L
conceived ...

Adam heard the words, but it took all his powers of concentration to make them sink in. "Are you sure?"

"I'm positive. They couldn't be anyone else's. I hadn't slept with anyone but you for over eighteen months before I conceived. I haven't been with another man since you."

"But the marriage...?"

"Was a sham." She made a statement of his question. "It was never consummated."

All the months he'd lain in that hospital, agonizing over her making love to another man, all the long nights when he'd survived on bitterness that she could forget him so easily.

Had she been clinging to the love they'd shared, resenting him, feeling betrayed as he had? But he could have never married someone else.

"Why didn't you tell me I was going to be a father? Why didn't you give me a chance to do right by you?"

JOANNA WAYNE

TRUMPED UP CHARGES

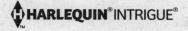

HARLEQUIN® INTRIGUE®

To my good friends Jean and John, who shared a wonderful week at the beach with my patient husband and me and put up with my preoccupation with writing this book.

Recycling programs
for this product may
not exist in your area.

ISBN-13: 978-0-373-69693-2

TRUMPED UP CHARGES

Printed in U.S.A.

www.Harlequin.com

ABOUT THE AUTHOR

Joanna Wayne was born and raised in Shreveport, Louisiana, and received her undergraduate and graduate degrees from LSU Shreveport. She moved to New Orleans in 1984, and it was there that she attended her first writing class and joined her first professional writing organization. Her debut novel, *Deep in the Bayou,* was published in 1994.

Now, dozens of published books later, Joanna has made a name for herself as being on the cutting edge of romantic suspense in both series and single-title novels. She has been on the Waldenbooks bestseller list for romance and has won many industry awards. She is also a popular speaker at writing organizations and local community functions and has taught creative writing at the University of New Orleans Metropolitan College.

Joanna currently resides in a small community forty miles north of Houston, Texas, with her husband. Though she still has many family and emotional ties to Louisiana, she loves living in the Lone Star State. You may write Joanna at P.O. Box 852, Montgomery, Texas 77356.

Books by Joanna Wayne

CAST OF CHARACTERS

Hadley O'Sullivan—When her twin daughters go missing, her secrets might be her worst enemy.

Adam Dalton—Hadley's former fiancé, who shows up at her door when her girls go missing.

Lacy and Lila O'Sullivan—Hadley's precocious twins.

RJ Dalton—Adam's father and the owner of Dry Gulch Ranch.

Matilda Bastion—Hadley's mother's longtime housekeeper.

Quinton Larson—Matilda's brother.

Alana and Sam Bastion—Matilda's sixteen-year-old daughter and eighteen-year-old son.

Kala—An accomplice in the kidnapping.

Janice O'Sullivan—Hadley's mother.

Detective Shelton Lane—The head detective on the kidnapping case.

Fred Casey—Professional hostage negotiator.

Durk and Meghan Lambert—RJ's neighbors.

Prologue

R. J. Dalton's days were numbered.

The prognosis pricked at him like a bull nettle. Nobody like a neurosurgeon to hand it to you straight. Not that he blamed the doc. Can't make a silk purse of a sow's belly.

R.J. eased up on the accelerator of his new Dodge Ram pickup and made the turn onto the familiar back road that led to Dry Gulch Ranch.

He didn't have any real gripes. He'd had seventy-eight years on this earth. For the most part, he'd lived them on his terms. He'd never backed down from a fight or walked away from a good time.

He wasn't always proud of what he'd done, but he'd never killed a man or got a woman pregnant he hadn't married—or at least offered to wed. The last wildcat he'd tangled with had told him what he could do with his proposal. Pretty as a new foal, but the woman had been all horns and rattles.

Not that Kiki or any of his exes would be coming around to plant daisies when he was belly-up under a plot of red Texas clay. Nobody even might show up for the funeral 'cept a few of his neighbors. Most of them would be there only to shoot the bull with the other pseudo mourners or to get the inside scoop on how to pick up the Dry Gulch for half its worth.

A man should have his funeral while he was still alive. That way he'd find out who his friends were. He'd also find out if any of his kids deserved a claim to the ranch that had been in his family for two generations.

"You should get your affairs in order as soon as possible."

That had been the doc's only solid advice. R.J.'s affairs had never been in order. He had no idea where to start now. He'd already offered to sell his land to the one family he fully trusted not to turn it into yet another golf course community or some noisy, high-traffic amusement park.

Hugh Lambert's beautiful widow, Carolina, had refused the offer. Told him he should leave the ranch to his kids. Hell, he didn't even know his kids and they'd given him no reason to believe they were interested in getting to know him. Probably more his fault than theirs, but it was what it was.

R.J. nudged his summer Stetson back an inch or two and stared at the passing scenery. Miles of barbed wire. Clusters of pecan trees. Grazing cattle. A tractor in the field, kicking up dust. All of it as familiar as his own face in his shaving mirror, yet somehow it looked different today.

The heat was the same, though. It rose in shimmering waves from the ribbon of asphalt that stretched in front of him. R.J. lowered the window and let his left elbow rest on the hot metal while the steamy Texas humidity slapped him in the face.

His thoughts slid back to the good old days when he'd been young and full of piss and vinegar. Back when his most pressing worries had centered on coming up with the entry fee for the next rodeo or checking out a firm-breasted buckle bunny.

If he'd thought about death at all then, he would have figured he'd get shot while slipping an ace from his sleeve or caught bonking another man's wife.

He'd never expected it to end with an inoperable tumor growing in his brain. Too bad he couldn't just saddle his horse now and ride off into the sunset like Randolph Scott used to do in the closing scenes of his movies.

Most folks around today didn't even know who Randolph Scott was. Worse, his own flesh and blood didn't even know who he was. Six kids. None of them would shed a tear when he died.

Leaving them a ranch and a few million dollars wouldn't change that—unless...

An idea popped into his head. It was unconventional. A tad devious. Pulling it off would require a good deal of underhanded scheming.

He liked it. He liked it a lot.

Chapter One

One month later

Adam Dalton pulled up behind a line of cars, pickup trucks and the Harley that blocked the driveway in front of the rambling ranch house. Judging from the number of vehicles, he'd guess all four of his half brothers and one half sister had also shown up for the reading of the will.

He'd never met any of his half siblings. The only reason he knew most of them existed was because their names and relationship were all listed in the letter he'd gotten inviting him to the ranch for this dubious occasion.

The legacy of Reuben Jackson Dalton.

R.J., the father he hadn't seen in twenty-seven years. All he knew of his biological father had come from his mother, Jerri, wife number three. If she'd ever said anything good about R.J., Adam didn't recall it.

But she must have loved him once—before she'd put him completely out of her life. She'd even lied about his being alive for years—which was strange in its own right, since she was normally a stickler for the truth.

She'd divorced R.J. when Adam was four years old.

He didn't remember a lot about that, but he did remember crying when they'd driven away from the ranch.

His mother had married again when Adam was eleven and Doug Abbott had become Adam's father in every way that mattered until he'd been killed in an early-morning pileup in a dense fog when Adam was eighteen. In his heart and mind, his father had died that day.

Still, Adam had always wondered about R.J. But from the time he was old enough to remember asking about him, his mother had told him R.J. had died soon after their divorce. He could tell she didn't like talking about him, so he'd eventually quit bringing up the subject.

Adam was twenty-one and leaving for his first tour of duty as a U.S. Marine before she admitted that R.J. was alive. Even then it was clear she hoped Adam wouldn't get in touch with him. She cautioned him that R. J. Dalton was nothing but trouble and had never cared anything about him or anyone else.

Nonetheless, Adam had thought about visiting R.J. then. He'd even gone so far as to get into his truck and start toward the ranch. He'd changed his mind before he'd reached the turnoff at Oak Grove. If R.J. had wanted him in his life, he'd have come looking for him. Adam would have been easy to find.

That's why the letter requesting his presence for the reading of the will had come as such a shock. He hadn't even heard that R.J. had died.

Oddly, Adam felt a twinge of loss as he opened the door to his truck and planted his feet on the hard earth. He wasn't sure if it was for R.J. or just for what might have been had R.J. ever been a real father to him.

But being overlooked by R.J. was only a precursor

to the rejection that had come later. Hadley O'Sullivan had seen to that.

While he'd been fighting for his life from injuries sustained in an ambush on a craggy mountainside in Afghanistan, she'd found a replacement lover. She'd married him and given birth to twins before Adam was even out of rehab. Apparently Hadley, like R.J., figured Adam was easy to forget.

All in the past, he reminded himself as he climbed the wide wooden steps to the house. The clamor of voices coming from behind the closed doors promised that this was not a friendly meeting. Dread punched him in the gut. He didn't need this.

His phone rang as he turned the doorknob. He checked the caller ID. It was his mother, no doubt wanting to know how the gathering of the clan was going. He ignored the call and turned his phone to vibrate.

Right now he just wanted to get the will reading over and done with. He'd expected nothing from R.J. while the man was alive. He didn't expect any more now, so how bad could the meeting be?

As soon as he took a seat, Attorney Conroe Phipps called the meeting to order and had the siblings introduce themselves. And then the fun started.

Phipps used his laser to point out each preposterous detail as he went over the requirements to receive a share of R.J.'s estate. The jolts came hard and fast, similar to an emotional earthquake with countless aftershocks.

Adam scanned the room, briefly studying each of his half siblings. They were clearly as stunned as he was.

Jade, the only female of the group, was kicking her crossed leg with a ferocity that made him think she was about to propel into orbit. Even Cannon, the rodeo cowboy of the group and the one person Adam thought might have been more receptive to the terms of the will, wore an expression that looked as if he'd been kicked by a bull.

No one was smiling. Adam himself swallowed a few curses along the way. He figured there would be time to vent his protests and frustrations once the long-winded attorney finished his spiel.

"To sum it up," Phipps said as he put down his laser, "in order to collect your share of the estate, you have to not only live on the ranch but take an active role in its operations for one full year."

Questions and arguments started flying with everybody talking at once. Phipps's only response to the chaos was a look of snide satisfaction, as if the uproar was exactly what he'd expected and possibly hoped for.

"I have a successful career. Do you honestly expect me to give that up to play cowboy?"

"How can we possibly all live here at once? It's a big house, but not that big."

"How much money are we talking about? Is there any oil involved?"

"If there's nothing but the ranch, why can't we just sell it and split the money? This much land so close to Dallas should be worth a small fortune."

"My mother was right. R. J. Dalton was nuts. I say we get our own attorney and prove he was mentally incompetent. There's no way I'm living out here in the middle of nowhere."

That last complaint had come from Jade who had stopped kicking and was now standing with her hands firmly planted on her hips.

Phipps clapped his hands loudly to get everyone's attention. "I know you have lots of questions, so I'm going to turn this meeting over to the man whom the money currently belongs to and whose last will and testament seem to be causing you so much distress."

He grinned and nodded toward a door that was opening behind him. "Come in, R.J., and meet your *loving* and *appreciative* family."

Mouths flew open, including Adam's, as an older, gray-haired man with ruddy, weathered skin and an eagle tattoo on his wrinkled right arm sauntered into the room.

Apparently R. J. Dalton was still very much alive. If there was any grief in the room after this, Adam figured R.J. would be the one dishing it out.

R.J. took his place at the front of the room and eyeballed each of his offspring in turn. He recognized all of them from current pictures he'd had his neighbor and former private investigator Meghan Lambert locate for him.

A few of his adult children showed a slight resemblance to him. Most didn't. But the most surprising thing was that they'd all shown up today and none had bolted and run yet even though they had no idea how much he was really worth.

"Guess you're surprised to see me here," he said, purposely exaggerating his Texas drawl. "Didn't see why I should send a corpse in my place and miss all the fun. But don't worry. According to my friendly neurosurgeon, I'll be lucky if I see the new year ring in."

To his children's credit, no one cheered at that pronouncement. But that could be because they were still in shock that he wasn't already dead as they'd been led to believe.

"I know it's only eleven in the morning, but this is Texas. There's beer, coffee and some of the best dad-gum barbecue this side of the Mississippi River in the kitchen."

"The kitchen we're all supposed to share for a year," someone grumbled.

"There's nothing in the will about sharing living quarters. There's a bunkhouse, a horse barn and a drafty old foreman's cabin on the property. I have to warn you, though, the cabin's starting to lean and the bunkhouse needs a new roof."

"And I suppose the horse barn is full of dead horses?" Jade quipped.

"Wrong. I got ten of the best damn thoroughbreds in the county and eight other good riding horses. I'm sure your mothers have told you that I've got a head as hard as a frozen wheel hub. That's all true. However I'm open to questions or just to chat. But I can assure you that the rules aren't going to change. So basically all you have to do is make up your mind. Do you want to be cut in or cut out?"

"To start, I think you should at least give us a ball-park figure as to the stakes we're talking about," Adam said.

"I reckon that's fair. We're talking about four hundred acres of prime ranchland that includes the house, outbuildings, about two hundred head of cattle and the horses I've already mentioned."

"What about cash and investments?" one of the guys asked.

"I'm worth about eight million dollars—give or take a few thousand."

Someone gave a low whistle. R.J. didn't see who, but he could tell from the way they all sat up a little straighter in their chairs that he had their attention.

R.J. saw no reason to mention that most of the money

had come from the one gamble in his life that had actually paid off for him—a one-dollar lottery ticket purchased from the truck stop in Oak Grove.

He winked and managed a smile. "I'm glad you all came and hopefully we might even discover we like or can at least tolerate each other. Now who wants a beer?"

THE OTHERS FOLLOWED R.J. to the kitchen. Adam stepped outside to clear his head.

So this is what it felt like to be bought. Was that what R.J. had done to his mother, insisted she dance to his tune or leave the party? Adam wondered how much it had been worth to the man to get rid of her and Adam.

He expected it was a sizable amount, enough to ease R.J.'s guilt if he'd had any. Even before Adam's mother had remarried, they'd lived in a nice house in an exclusive neighborhood and as far as he knew, there had never been any money worries. His mother still lived in that house.

His phone vibrated. This time he took the call. "Hello, Mom. What's the matter? Can't wait to hear about R.J.'s latest tricks?"

"Did you hear the AMBER Alert the Houston police issued a couple of hours ago?" Her voice was shaking so hard he could barely understand her.

"I haven't."

"Twin girls were kidnapped from their grandmother's home in a Dallas subdivision during the night."

"Is this someone you know?"

"The grandmother is Janice O'Sullivan, Adam. It was Hadley's children who were kidnapped."

His heart bucked and knocked against his chest wall. He fumbled for words while he tried to get his mind around the news. "How did that happen?"

"I have no idea. The only details released were a description of the girls and the area where they were kidnapped."

"Then how do you know the missing girls are Hadley's daughters?"

"My friend Crystal just called. Her daughter's husband is on the Dallas police force and was one of the first responders to the 911 call. He talked to Hadley. She's frantic."

"I'm sure."

"I know you two had a bitter breakup, son, but her daughters are missing. I think you should go over there and see if you can help."

"She has the Dallas police and maybe even the FBI. I'm sure they don't need me."

"But you're a decorated marine."

"We didn't handle child abductions in Afghanistan, Mom. Besides there's no reason to think Hadley or her husband would appreciate my interference."

"There was no husband around when Crystal's son-in-law talked to her. She was by herself."

"Where was her mother?"

"Janice is in the hospital. She's having surgery this morning. That's why Hadley and the girls are in town. And now her girls have been kidnapped. Hadley can't face this all alone."

"She has a husband."

"But he's not with her now and who knows how long it will take him to get to Dallas. I don't even know where they live. But you're here, Adam. At least talk to her. You've always helped anyone in trouble."

But this wasn't anyone. This was the woman whose image he'd held on to through hell and back only to learn she'd married someone else and borne his children.

The woman he'd spent the past few years trying to erase from his heart and mind.

But Hadley was alone and no doubt terrified, her children in the hands of an abductor. His heart pounded as adrenaline exploded inside him.

She might kick him out when he got there, but not going to her wasn't even an option. Eight million or eighty million dollars on the line, it made no difference.

He was out of here.

Chapter Two

"When did you first realize your daughters were missing?"

"When I woke up and went into their room." Hadley stared at Detective Shelton Lane, trying her best to concentrate and cooperate. But his questions were redundant and tearing at her slivered control.

"I've explained this at least three times this morning to three different police officers. Don't you talk to each other?"

"I'm sorry to put you through this, but I was just assigned to the case, Ms. O'Sullivan. I like to get my answers firsthand."

"So you just sit here and ask me the same questions over and over instead of looking for my girls?"

"We've issued an AMBER Alert. Every officer on the street has your daughters' picture. I have officers going house to house in this neighborhood talking to everyone who might have seen something."

"I just want my girls back." Tears welled in her eyes. She dabbed at them with the shredded tissue clutched in her hand.

Detective Lane granted her a few seconds to gain control before he hit her with the next question. "Were you home all evening?"

"The girls went with me when I drove Mother to the hospital. We stayed until she was settled in her room. It was just after five when we got home. We didn't leave again after that."

"And no one else was here with you?"

"No one. I made the girls dinner and then we went outside so they could get a little exercise before baths and bedtime."

Hadley stood and walked to the window, looking out over the front walk where Lacy and Lila had ridden their trikes last night. They'd been so cute. So happy. So innocent.

Had someone been watching even then and planning the abduction? The front door had been unlocked while they were outside, but she'd been right there. She'd surely have seen if anyone had entered the house.

She turned away from the window. "This is supposed to be a safe neighborhood. There are guards at the gate. I don't see how this could have happened."

"I'm having trouble figuring that out myself." The detective shifted in his seat. "You say you didn't hear anything during the night."

"Nothing. And it's not as if I slept that well. I was worried."

"About the girls?"

"About my mother. I told you, she's in surgery right now, having a malignant stomach tumor removed. I was supposed to be with her. Now…" Now she was in a nightmare.

"Did you check on them during the night?"

"Once."

"What time was that?"

"It was a few minutes after one. Eleven after, to be exact. I remember looking at the clock when I woke up.

They were both sleeping soundly. I picked up the almost full glass of water Lila had asked for when I was reading them a bedtime story last night and carried the glass to the kitchen."

"What did you do with the glass?"

"It's probably still on the counter. What difference does it make?"

"I'm just trying to get a complete picture in my mind. So you put Lila's glass on the table, went back to bed and then you didn't go back to their bedroom until this morning?"

"Right."

"Did you go to check on them as soon as you woke?"

"I went to the bathroom first, but then I went to get them up."

"When you didn't find them there, what did you do?"

"I called for them and searched the house." Hadley dropped to a chair and tried to get a handle on the sickening fear that was churning inside her.

"How long did you look for them before you called 911?"

"I'm not sure. I think it was only fifteen minutes or so. By that time I was shaking so hard that I couldn't punch in the numbers. Matilda took the phone and did it for me."

"I thought you said you were alone."

"I was. Matilda arrived while I was searching for the girls. She helped and even searched the garage and the yard."

"And Matilda is your mother's housekeeper?"

So he had talked to the other officers. "Yes. Matilda Bastion. She's worked for Mother for years. She's practically part of the family."

"Where is Matilda now?"

"At the hospital. When I couldn't leave, she went to be with Mother."

Thoughts of her mother attacked anew Hadley's fragile hold on control. Janice was still in surgery, but unless they found the girls quickly, she'd have to be told about the abduction. As if cancer wasn't enough to deal with.

"Who was going to watch your daughters while you were at the hospital this morning?"

"Matilda. They were excited about staying with her. She's so good with them."

"Does Matilda have a key to the house?"

Hadley nodded, but even in her fractured emotional state she could see where this was going. "Matilda had nothing to do with the abduction."

"I'm just making sure we have the facts straight."

Hadley checked her watch for the hundredth time that morning. It was five before twelve. Lunchtime for the girls. Were they hungry? Were they crying for her? Were they safe?

A new wave of anxiety coursed through her veins. "What kind of monster would take two little girls from their beds in the middle of the night?"

"I don't know, but I can assure you that we're doing everything in our power to find out."

The doorbell rang. The jarring noise splintered Hadley's rattled nerves. She hesitated for a heartbeat and then jumped up and ran to the door, praying it was a police officer bringing Lacy and Lila home.

She swung open the door and stared into the face of the last person she'd expected to see. Her muscles clenched. Resentment and old hurts attacked with dizzying force. Her hand clutched the door, ready to slam it in his face.

"Hadley."

The sound of her name on his lips reached deep inside her, striking chords she didn't want to acknowledge.

He opened his arms and her traitorous, angst-stricken body fell into the only port in this terrifying storm.

HADLEY'S HOT TEARS fell on Adam's neck and rolled beneath the collar of his shirt. His reaction hit hard and fast, his senses reeling from the fragrance of her hair, the softness of her skin.

Damn. How could he think of that now? He was here to help. Start getting caught up in the good, the bad and the ugly of the past and that would be impossible.

A man about his age in navy blue slacks and a white sports shirt stepped into view behind Hadley. The girls' father, no doubt, the man who'd swept Hadley off her feet and helped her move on in record time.

The one whose neck should be catching her tears.

Adam disentangled himself from Hadley quickly and extended a hand to the man.

"Adam Dalton. Hadley and I go way back. I heard about the abduction and came to see if I could do anything to help."

"This is Detective Shelton Lane," Hadley said.

So he wasn't the husband. Still his handshake was far from friendly and his gaze and stance were clearly meant to be intimidating. Adam wasn't fazed. It was hard to bully a former marine.

"How did you hear about the abduction?" Lane asked.

"It made the news."

"No names were given in the AMBER release."

"Police leak," Adam quipped honestly. "You know how fast those travel."

The detective scowled.

"I'm not here to interfere in the search," Adam assured him. "I'm just here to offer my support. Do you have a problem with that?"

"I don't, but it's not my house."

Adam turned back to Hadley. "I'd like to help if I can, but say the word and I'm out of here."

"You're here. You may as well stay. Maybe you can come up with something we haven't."

He doubted it. He knew about raiding terrorist hideouts and sneaking past enemy lines on craggy mountainsides. He knew nothing of tracking down a kidnapper of innocent children.

But then he did have a reputation for being a whiz at eking out danger.

Hadley led them to a small sitting room off the foyer.

"I'll make some coffee," she said.

The detective brushed her offer aside. "Can that wait? I only have a few more questions."

"What good does it do to keep going over and over the same information? There's nothing more I can tell you. If I had any idea who took Lacy and Lila, I'd have screamed his name the second you walked in or gone after the monster myself."

Lane spread his hands in front of him, palms up. "I understand your frustration, Ms. O'Sullivan. But try to bear with me a few more minutes."

The detective had referred to her by her maiden name. Odd, since she was married. But then the detective's focus was surely on more important matters than getting her name straight.

"Any problem with my listening in?" Adam asked.

"That's up to Ms. O'Sullivan."

"Stay," Hadley said. "Then you won't have to ask the same questions when the detective leaves." She dropped into an upholstered chair by the window and took a tissue from the box on the table.

The detective took a chair near Hadley's. That left the sofa for Adam. Before they could get started, the detective's phone rang.

"I need to take this in private," he said, "but I'll only be a minute." He hurried out of the room.

"I hate to ask, but can you bring me up to speed?" Adam asked. "Just the basics for now."

"All I know are the basics." The terror was not only etched in her eyes but echoed in every syllable.

"The twins and I stayed here alone last night because Mother had to check in the hospital yesterday afternoon. She's in surgery now, having a malignant tumor removed from her stomach. When I woke up this morning, the girls weren't in their bedrooms. We searched the house frantically, calling for them, but they weren't here."

"You said we," Adam noted. "Who was with you?"

"Matilda Bastion, Mother's housekeeper. She got here just after I realized the girls weren't in their room. Someone broke into the house and carried them off, Adam. I should have heard them. I should have saved…." She choked on the self-incrimination, swallowing the end of her lament.

"Except, technically there's no sign of a break-in," Lane said as he reentered the room.

"What exactly does that mean?" Adam questioned.

"According to Ms. O'Sullivan, the doors and windows were still locked this morning. The alarm system wasn't set, and it didn't go off during the night."

"I don't remember setting it last night," Hadley said. "I had so much on my mind."

"But the abductor would have expected it to go off, unless he had the code to disarm it before it did."

"Or the technical ability to disarm it from the outside," Adam said.

"That's possible," Lane admitted. "But the evidence still suggests that whoever took Lacy and Lila either had a key or was let in and out by someone on the inside."

"No one let him in," Hadley said. "I was the only one here."

"Which leaves us with an abductor with a key to the house."

That added a multitude of new layers of complexity to the situation, Adam decided. On the positive side, it narrowed the field of suspects. They just had to figure out who had a key to the house and the means, opportunity, motive and perhaps a rap sheet.

Other than the arrest records, the information would have to come from Janice O'Sullivan. He was certain Hadley would hate dragging her mother into this so soon after surgery, but she'd have no other options—unless they found the girls first.

Adam listened as the detective went back to his questions for Hadley. Most dealt with her search for the girls and anything unusual she or Matilda had noticed. A few dealt with Hadley's personal relationships and whether anyone had stalked or threatened her.

There was no mention of Hadley's husband. His whereabouts and their relationship had likely been covered before Adam arrived on the scene.

This time it was a call on Hadley's cell phone that interrupted the conversation. She yanked it from her pocket and checked the caller ID. Disappointment furrowed deep grooves into her forehead. Clearly this was not the kidnapper.

"It's Matilda, calling from the hospital," she said.

"Answer it," the detective said, "but don't stay on the line long. We don't want to miss a call from the kidnapper."

Hadley talked for only a few seconds, but Adam could tell from her side of the conversation that the call wasn't good news. He didn't get a chance to ask before she lit into the detective.

"Matilda was in tears," Hadley said. "A cop just left there and he treated her as if she was involved in the girls' disappearance."

"I'm sure he didn't accuse her of any criminal involvement."

"Perhaps not directly, but he definitely insinuated it."

"Everyone who has a key to this house is a person of interest, Ms. O'Sullivan. *Everyone.*"

"That's ridiculous. Matilda has babysat the girls since they were only a few months old. She'd never hurt them. She loves them."

"I hope you're right, but I can't afford that kind of trust in this case and frankly, neither can you."

Adam agreed, though he didn't comment.

"That's enough questions for now," Lane said. "I need to check on a few things with headquarters. Why don't you and Adam go have that coffee?"

"What if my phone rings and I don't know the caller?"

"Don't answer it without finding me first so I can listen in. I'll be in my car."

She nodded her agreement.

Lane stood and left the room, leaving Adam and Hadley alone. Awkward tension swelled, almost as tangible a presence as the detective had been.

Adam struggled to think of the right thing to say and do. He'd take action over dealing with emotions any day.

Finally, Hadley broke the stalemate. She squared her shoulders and turned to face him. "I didn't expect to ever see you again."

"I kind of figured the same."

"So why did you come?"

Good question, and he wasn't even sure he knew the real answer. "I knew you'd be devastated and desperate," he said, settling on an obvious truth. "I'd really like to help if I can, but if my being here makes it worse, I'll leave."

Hadley stared at the floor for long seconds, her arms hugged tightly about her chest, before she finally looked up and met his gaze. "I'm not sure what I want, Adam. I'm not sure of anything right now."

"It's still your call."

"Let's discuss it over coffee."

It wasn't the warmest welcome he'd ever received, but he could work with it. There was no time to waste. Every second the girls were missing made it less likely they'd be found alive. Hadley wasn't stupid. Deep down, she had to know that as well.

The clock was ticking. The cops had their way of doing things. Adam had his, honed through his years of active duty when he'd learned not to trust anyone except his fellow marines and to always have a plan of action.

And right now, he had no plan.

HADLEY WATCHED AS ADAM picked up a framed photo in the room the girls had shared last night.

"This has to be the twins," he commented.

A knot formed in her throat as she nodded.

"Which is which?"

"The one on the right holding her doll by the hair is Lila."

"I don't see how you tell them apart."

"Some people can't, but it's easy for me. There are lots of subtle differences. Lila's hair is curlier and her cheeks are fuller. And she carries that wiry-headed doll everywhere she goes. Lacy has a scar just below her right ear where she fell on a rock while chasing a squirrel when she was first learning to walk. She's the daring one. And her eyes are the most remarkable shade of blue-green I've ever seen."

"Like yours. Both girls definitely take after you."

"That's what everyone says."

And yet she saw their father whenever she looked at them. In any other situation she would have never let Adam back into her life. But the thought of being in this house alone when the detective left was unbearable.

Even with Adam beside her, just being in this room was difficult. Her insides were in such upheaval, she could barely function. Adam, on the other hand, seemed totally focused. As soon as she'd started the coffee, he'd asked to see this room.

He'd examined the window from top to bottom first and then stared at each bed as if he thought it would cough up images of what had occurred here last night.

He returned the picture to the shelf and stooped to get a closer look at a stain on the carpet.

"Was this here before?"

"I'm not sure," she admitted. "Why?"

"I noticed a similar one on the hall carpet. Seems kind of odd since the rest of the carpet is spotless."

"Mother is fastidious. She usually has the carpet cleaned professionally as soon as we leave. Not that she doesn't love having us here, dirt and all."

Adam continued to study the stain. "This doesn't look like dirt."

"What do you think it is?"

"Could be oil that someone smeared in an attempt for a fast cleanup."

"That looks too dark to be oil and I know no one's been cooking in here."

"Haven't been working on cars, either, I'd guess, though this looks like the kind of stain you'd find on a garage floor."

"Do you think the stain was left by the abductor?"

"Could be."

"Hard to believe he was brazen enough to stick around long enough to clean up a stain from his shoes."

"Only if he thought it would incriminate him," Adam agreed.

"More likely the cops or CSI guys checking for fingerprints tracked it in," Hadley said.

"Hopefully they found lots of usable prints," Adam said, changing the subject. "If they did, they could have the kidnapper in custody and the girls safely in hand before the sun goes down."

Hadley didn't know if Adam actually believed that or was only trying to calm her. She believed it. She had to. It was all she had to hold on to.

"I'm sure the coffee is ready," she said.

"Go ahead and get yours. I'll join you in a few minutes. I'd like to look around outside first."

Hadley led the way. As it turned out there was not one, but two more stains similar to the one in the bedroom. They didn't look like fresh stains to Hadley, but as Adam pointed out, that could be the result of someone trying to hastily remove them and failing at the task. She'd talk to Detective Lane and ask if he'd tested the stains.

The kitchen door opened onto a covered deck. When they reached it, Hadley turned the dead bolt and then the key.

Adam took a second look at the dead bolt. "Is there any way the girls could have unlocked the door themselves and wandered outside?"

"No, though they're smart and adventurous enough to try it, especially Lacy. When they're here we keep the doors locked and the keys out of reach. We keep this key in the salt keeper." Hadley pointed to the antique container resting on an open display shelf near the door.

"Good plan. And the key was still there this morning when the girls went missing?"

"All the keys were out of reach and all the doors were still locked, as were all the windows. That's why I was so certain they must be hiding in the house."

"How many doors are there?"

"Three. One opens to the garage through the laundry room. The abductor definitely didn't come in that way. I know I would have woken had the garage door opened."

"Did the house show signs of being burglarized?"

"No. Nothing was out of place, not even in the room where the Lacy and Lila were sleeping. But I should have heard something."

"Unless he drugged them while they were sleeping so that they wouldn't wake up?" Adam said.

Her precious daughters drugged and stolen away from her. She shuddered as icy fingers tightened around her heart.

Adam put a hand on her shoulder.

His touch was no doubt meant to calm her, but it had the opposite effect. She blinked hard, trying to stop the tears that burned in the corners of her eyes from escaping and starting an avalanche she wouldn't be able to stop.

She lingered near the back door as Adam stepped onto the spacious, covered deck. For the first time since he'd arrived, she took a good look at him.

He'd changed in three years. He was leaner than before with an edge of hardness to the angles and planes of his face that made him look every one of his thirty-one years. That took nothing away from his rugged good looks.

But he was far more than outward appearance. He was his own man, a hero who'd won medals for his courage under fire. He never walked away from danger or risk.

But he was only a man. She turned and walked away, before she started expecting too much.

She filled a mug with strong, black coffee and rummaged the drawer next to the sink for a pad and pencil. Dropping them onto the island, she slid onto a kitchen barstool.

After a few sips of coffee, she jotted down a title for her list.

People Who Had Keys to the House.

Hadley couldn't make a definitive list before her mother recovered from the anesthetics and could think clearly, but she could have some prospects ready that might jar her mother's memory.

The first name she wrote was Matilda Bastion. She had a key, but she would never do anything to hurt Lila or Lacy.

Neighbors made the number-two spot. Hadley couldn't possibly list all of them by name, but her very social mother knew everyone on the block and might have given any one of them a key to check on the house when she was away.

The third spot fell to Ally Fritz. Ally was a decorator who'd overseen the kitchen remodeling last year and kept a close eye on the construction workers. There was a good chance she'd been given a key. She was trustworthy, but the key might have been left lying around her shop.

And who knew how many unnamed others Hadley might have never met? Her mother had frequent guests and often hired caterers for her social functions.

Someone with a key who knew Hadley and the girls were spending the night last night. Someone who was in desperate need of money.

She had to believe the abduction was about collecting a ransom. Any other motive was too frightening to bear.

But why didn't the kidnapper call?

A coughing noise startled her. She looked up, expecting Adam but seeing the detective instead.

"The wiretap is in place," Lane said, "just as we talked about. If the kidnapper calls, I'll get it simultaneously. Agree to anything, but demand to talk to both Lacy and Lila. Stay as calm as you can and keep him on the phone as long as you can. Once he breaks the connection, I'll get in touch with you immediately."

"Are both my cell phone and the house phone tapped?"

"Yes, but I took the liberty of having the house calls forwarded to your cell phone so that you won't miss a call when you're at the hospital."

"Thanks. I was going to ask you about that."

"I assume you'll be leaving for the hospital soon."

"Within the next fifteen minutes. I hate to leave here, yet I need to be there when Mother comes out of recovery. I can't take a chance on someone else telling her about the kidnapping."

"You do realize that I'll have to question her as soon as the doctor agrees to it."

"Can't you just give me the questions you have and let me ask her? Talking to the police is only going to upset her more."

"I'm sorry. Investigations don't work that way."

"They work however you say they work."

"Is there a problem in here?" This time the voice was Adam's.

"I don't have one," Lane said, his stare leveled at Hadley.

"I'll do my best not to upset your mother, Ms. O'Sullivan, but right now she's our best hope for identifying the kidnapper quickly."

"I understand."

Only she didn't. She didn't understand any of this. She should be at the hospital with her mother. Lacy and Lila should be here with Matilda, playing with their toys or watching one of their favorite animated movies.

This nightmare should not be happening.

Lane let himself out and Adam helped himself to coffee. "Did Lane say something to upset you?"

"Why do you ask?"

"Your eyes were shooting daggers at him when I interrupted your conversation."

"I don't like his attitude at times. I want to believe he's doing everything he can to find Lacy and Lila, but he talks of rules and procedures. My girls' lives are at stake and he can't give an inch."

Adam walked over and sidled onto the stool next to hers. "I'm sure he's aware of what you're going through. I'll wager the whole department is using every weapon in their arsenal to find Lacy and Lila. Missing kids are always top priority for the police."

"So you think I'm being unreasonable?"

"Actually, I think you're doing an amazing job of handling this."

"Well, you're wrong. I'm crazy inside. I want to scream and kick and beat my fists against the wall."

"Go ahead if it helps. You can even use me for a punching bag."

"Careful what you offer."

"I always am."

And she'd never been careful enough. She downed the last few sips of her coffee and then slid the mug away. "I can't just sit here and do nothing. I'm going to the hospital."

"Do you want company?"

She wanted to shout no. She didn't want to need him. The refusal wouldn't come.

"It's up to you," she said.

"Then I'd like to tag along, but I have one question first."

"I'm sick of being interrogated. All I've done all morning is answer the same questions over and over as if they expect my answers to change."

"I need to ask anyway."

"Then get it over with."

"Where is the twins' father?"

Chapter Three

The silence lasted so long that Adam thought Hadley might not answer at all. He saw no reason why she'd object. Under the circumstances, it was a legitimate concern and required only a simple, direct response.

Adam rephrased the question. "Is your husband on his way to Dallas?"

"No." Hadley picked up her mug, took it to the sink and held it under the spray. "He won't be coming," she said, without looking at Adam.

The answer stunned him. "Why not?"

"Does it matter?" She picked up a sponge and began to buff the impeccably clean and shining granite countertop. She worked strenuously, her fear and frustration fueling the task.

He'd pushed too far. She was vulnerable, too emotionally fragile to be pushed on a subject she clearly didn't want to talk about.

He carried his cup to the sink. "Enough said. I was out of line in putting you on the spot."

"You didn't, but why go into something that's not relevant when the situation is already overwhelming?"

"None of my business anyway. Let's get out of here."

"I'll get my handbag."

Adam couldn't imagine any valid excuse for Hadley's husband not getting here as fast as he could. Even if he and Hadley were having marital problems, no halfway decent father would ignore the plight of his missing daughters—unless…

Unless the guy was involved in the crime.

The detective had stressed that *everyone* was a suspect. Was there a chance he'd had the twins' father in mind when he'd made that point? Could this abduction be connected to a bitter divorce and custody battle?

If it was, a lot of unexplained issues suddenly made sense. The man could easily have a key to his mother-in-law's house. And the girls could have just gone back to sleep without a fuss if they woke up and found themselves in their daddy's arms.

But there were two significant problems with that scenario. Hadley's panic and terror were too real for her not to believe the girls were in real and imminent danger. If she feared her husband were behind that, she surely would have told the cops to go after him.

It was difficult to imagine that a man could ever hurt his own children, but it happened. All fathers were not created equal. No one knew that better than Adam. R.J. hadn't been physically abusive. He simply hadn't been around. The scars he'd inflicted were invisible.

Apparently R.J. wanted to play catch-up now. The old reprobate was probably worried about facing his maker and trying to atone for a few of his sins. He couldn't even do that without manipulating the situation and attempting to screw up his children's lives.

Hadley returned and Adam pulled his keys from his pocket. The saga of R.J. and his latest scheme would be continued later—when Lacy and Lila were safe.

MATILDA SAT IN the back of the small hospital chapel, her hands folded in her lap. She didn't pray like her friends at the neighborhood church did. Some might not call what she did praying at all.

Mostly she just liked to sit in the quiet and envision God's arms wrapped around her to comfort and guide her. Today her thoughts were so troubled that nothing could calm her spirit. It might go down as the worst day of her life and that was saying a lot.

She closed her eyes and focused her thoughts on Janice O'Sullivan. Janice believed they were friends. Matilda never saw it that way. The gulf between employer and employee was too wide, especially from her side.

It wasn't simply that Janice was the boss. It was more about the money and the lifestyle. Janice had all she could ever want. Matilda struggled every week to make ends meet.

Not that Janice didn't pay her a fair salary. It was well above minimum wage and she provided generous Christmas bonuses, as well. She'd even bought Matilda a new washer and dryer last year when hers went out.

Janice's husband had died of a heart attack five years ago and left her an extremely profitable investment portfolio, a paid-for house worth over a million dollars in a posh Dallas neighborhood and a sizable life insurance payout.

Matilda's husband, Brent, had been shot and killed when he'd inadvertently walked into an armed robbery in process. He'd stopped at the convenience store after he'd left the night shift at a local plant. He had no insurance and no savings. At the time, Matilda had no employable skills and two young children under the age of eight.

Janice's only daughter was a jewel, thoughtful of her and a model mother to those precious girls. Matilda's daughter was only sixteen, but she was also pure joy. She was an honor student and on the school cheerleading squad.

Her eighteen-year-old son, Sam, was the rebel. He'd never gotten into any real trouble the way her brother, Quinton, had at that age, but he was resentful and eternally pushing Matilda's rules. He was attending summer school now just so he could replace the fake graduation certificate they'd awarded him for a real one.

So, even though Matilda liked Janice and appreciated what she'd done for her and her family, they weren't bosom buddies.

But they were close enough that Matilda really hoped the morning's surgery would leave Janice cancer-free. Good news on that front would be a huge relief, but it would be overshadowed by the twins' disappearance.

But the tragedy wouldn't devastate Janice the way it might some. She had more spunk and grit than a prize-fighter. Matilda envied her that.

She stood and slipped quietly out of the chapel. New anxiety struck the second she got off the fourth-floor elevator. Officer Grummet, the cop who'd given her the third degree earlier, stood in the hallway just past the nurses' station.

She'd had enough of him and his accusatory tone. He hadn't directly called her a suspect but his mannerisms and pointed questions had made it clear that he suspected she knew more than she was saying.

She'd always been a rotten liar.

Grummet started walking in her direction, but his gaze was focused on the shapely nurse who was standing at a patient's room door a few feet in front of him.

Matilda ducked into an empty room and waited until he'd passed and had ample time to board the elevator.

She was only a few feet from Janice's room when she heard a familiar voice. She turned to find Hadley rushing toward her, a nice-looking man keeping pace. Hadley pulled Matilda into a heart-wrenching hug that had Matilda struggling to hold back tears.

"Any news?" Matilda asked when Hadley's arms dropped back to her side.

"None. No leads and no contact from the kidnapper."

"That will come," Matilda said, expressing more hope than confidence.

Hadley stepped closer to the man. Matilda figured he was a detective, since she was pretty sure that Hadley wasn't in a relationship. Janice frequently lamented the fact that Hadley showed no interest in having a man in her life.

"Have you seen Mother?" Hadley asked. "Is she awake?"

"I can't say. She was still in recovery when I went down to the cafeteria for coffee and a sandwich. After that I stopped in the chapel for a few minutes. I'm on my way back to her room now."

"Did you by any chance talk to Dr. Gates after surgery?"

"No," Matilda said. "The nurse said he'd talk to you when you got here. Are you going to tell Janice about the abduction?"

"Yes. I hate it, but she's the only one who can give us the names of everyone who has a key to her house."

"She'll handle it," Matilda assured her. "When the going gets tough, your mother is always tougher. And far better she hear it from you than from anyone else."

"I know. But I'd hoped she wouldn't have to hear it at all. I keep praying the police will call and tell me that they've arrested the kidnapper and that Lacy and Lila are safe and on their way home."

"You keep on praying and trusting in the Lord, Hadley. Half the city of Dallas is praying right along with you. Even the ones who don't pray are on the lookout for your two sweethearts ever since that first AMBER Alert was released. People around here come together in a crisis. That's the Texas way."

"I know," Hadley said. "You'd think the cops would have a decent lead by now."

Dread swelled inside Matilda like a pot of soaking beans. "If you don't need me anymore, I think I'll go home for a while."

"Of course. You should. I'll be okay. I have Adam." She touched the man's arm. "Sorry I didn't introduce him sooner, but this is Adam Dalton, an old friend. Adam, this is Matilda Bastion."

Matilda recognized the name immediately. She'd never met Adam, but she knew that he and Hadley had been engaged for a few months several years back. Janice had never approved of the relationship and Matilda figured she'd had something to do with their breakup.

She sized him up while they exchanged a greeting. The fact that he was standing by Hadley in a time of crisis was good enough for Matilda.

She looked up as a middle-aged nurse approached them.

"Is one of you Hadley O'Sullivan?"

"I am," Hadley answered.

"Dr. Gates would like to speak to you. He'll meet you in your mother's room."

Matilda said a quick goodbye and made her exit. If this was bad news, she didn't want to hear it. Today was already hell enough.

HADLEY LOOKED UP as the doctor joined them in her mother's room. She was only vaguely aware of Adam standing beside her, but glad he was there. His strength and confidence worked like an invisible conductor to fight off hysteria and keep her at least semi-grounded.

"The surgery was a success," Dr. Gates said calmly. "The tumor was larger than the scans indicated, requiring more involved and complex incisions, but it wasn't attached to any vital organs."

"That is great news." She leaned against the bed frame. "Will she need follow-up chemo or radiation treatments?"

"Your oncologist will go over that with you when he gets the full results back from tissue samples taken from surrounding areas. Your mother tolerated the surgery well, but with her blood pressure problems, I'd like to keep her in the hospital for at least three nights. I've already cleared that with the insurance company."

"Now you'll only have to convince Mother."

"I'm hoping you can help persuade her. She's a very lucky woman to have caught this in time."

Lucky.

Under the circumstances, the word seemed so ludicrous as to be vile. Yesterday, the news he'd just given her would have been cause for celebration. Today it barely penetrated the layers of horror.

"Is Mother alert?" she asked.

"She's coming out from under the influence of the anesthetics, but I want her to stay as quiet and as calm as possible for at least the next twenty-four hours. That means no visits from those precocious granddaughters she was telling me about."

"I'm afraid there's a problem with keeping her calm," Hadley said. Her insides began to churn again and for a few seconds she was afraid she was going to have to make a run for the bathroom or risk throwing up on the floor.

While she struggled to settle her nerves, Adam took over for her. He explained the situation to the doctor much more succinctly than she could have managed.

Shock shattered the doctor's professional demeanor. "Someone broke into your house while you were sleeping and abducted both of your daughters? That's..." He paused, evidently struggling for the right word. "It's evil, depraved beyond comprehension. What kind of maniac would do such a thing?"

"Apparently, one with a key to Janice O'Sullivan's house," Adam explained. "No door or window locks were tampered with."

"That's why I have to tell Mother the truth," Hadley said. "I have to ask her for the names of everyone who could possibly have gotten their hands on a key."

"You're right," Dr. Gates agreed. "Her input is invaluable. Even if it weren't, she'd never forgive you for not telling her the truth immediately."

"How long before she'll be coherent enough for me to explain the situation and ask her about the key?"

"She'll be able to communicate within the hour though she will still demonstrate signs of the drugs." He scratched his chin thoughtfully. "I need to be in the room with you when you tell her about the kidnapping."

"Are you afraid the shock could cause Mother to suffer a heart attack?"

"I'm a grandfather," Dr. Gates said. "I haven't had

surgery and I'm in perfect health. I'd be in danger of having a heart attack if someone kidnapped one of my grandchildren, much less two."

"I'll make sure you're in the room when I tell her," Hadley said. "But that won't be the end of it. Detective Shelton Lane is heading up the case and he's already bugging me about questioning Mother."

"That's up to you," Gates said. "But if it were me, I'd insist that a family member be in the room during any police visits, at least for the next twenty-four hours. Your mother, while cognizant, will still be under the influence of the anesthetics."

"But if she can help find the girls in any way, I want her to be heard."

"That's why I recommend having a family member with her during the meeting. There's a difference between questioning and harassment. The detective on this case may be the exception, but unfortunately, some cops don't differentiate between the two very well. At least that's been my experience with other patients."

"Sounds like a good idea to me," Adam said.

"Yes, but I'm not sure I can call those shots," Hadley said.

"I can," Dr. Gates said. "If you want, I can leave an order with the nursing staff that says positively no visitors except you or someone you accompany."

Hadley hesitated. She didn't want to interfere with the investigation. She wanted the girls found. And it wasn't as if her mother was a suspect.

"I think you should do as Dr. Gates suggests," Adam encouraged.

"Okay," she agreed, "but add Matilda Bastion to the list of people who can visit without me present."

"Spell that last name for me, just to make sure I get it right on the order."

She did and they talked for a minute more before the door opened and her mother was wheeled into the room. Hadley stood aside while her mother was transferred from the gurney to her bed.

She appeared groggy, her eyes narrow slits beneath puffy lids. Her usually well-coiffed hair was damp and pressed against her head.

She saw Hadley and smiled. Then her gaze moved to Adam. The smile vanished.

"Whass see doin' here?" Her words were slurred but clear enough that they all got the message that she wasn't happy to see him.

Hadley breathed a sigh of relief. Neither drugs nor pain would keep Janice O'Sullivan from coming to the brawl ready to fight. She'd stave off the effects of the drugs and give them the names they needed. Detective Lane and the DPD could do the rest.

Lacy and Lila might be home in time for her to tuck them into bed tonight.

THE LATE-AFTERNOON SUN was almost blinding as Hadley and Adam made their way across the hospital parking lot. Hadley slowed her pace to reach in her handbag for her sunglasses.

She put them on and adjusted the frame on the bridge of her nose. The glare diminished. Her desperation intensified. They'd spent an hour with her mother privately before the detective had joined them for a rehash of the same information. The illuminating moment that could change everything had never come.

Now, thanks to powerful medication, her mother was

resting and in the hands of the private nurse they'd hired and the competent fourth-floor nursing team.

"I had such high hopes for Mother coming up with a name that would make sense of the abduction and lead us to the girls. Now it seems that's just another dead end."

"Don't count it out yet. Lane said he'd follow up on the construction workers who'd been involved in her remodeling project."

"He didn't sound encouraged that construction workers were the best suspects we could come up with. Especially since the remodeling project has been finished for at least six months and Lacy and Lila had never been there when they were working."

"Every lead is important," Adam said. "Your mother may come up with more names when the meds wear off a bit."

"She'll definitely try," Hadley said.

"I'm sure," Adam said as they reached the truck. "I thought for a minute there she was going to jump out of that hospital bed, grab an AK-47 and storm every house in Dallas until she found the girls."

"Too bad Lane's team isn't doing that."

"I'm sure they're throwing everything they have into this, Hadley. Missing children are top priority on every police force in America."

He opened her door for her and then rounded the truck and slid behind the wheel.

Hadley had to admit that her mother had taken the news like the fighter she was. She'd ordered the nurse to get her clothes and dared anyone to try and stop her from leaving the hospital.

A failed attempt to sit up by herself had allowed Dr. Gates and Hadley to convince her that the best way she could help was to provide them with information. She'd tried and then become furious at herself when she couldn't give them what they needed.

To the detective's credit, he hadn't harassed her mother. In fact he'd been almost too accommodating and a lot of his time had been wasted on idle chatter. At least it had seemed that way to Hadley.

"Did you find the detective's interaction with Mother odd?" she asked as Adam backed from the parking spot.

"You mean the fact that he talked more about you and your relationship to your mother and to the girls than he did about people with access to the house?"

"Exactly."

Hadley's cell phone rang. Her pulse pounded—until she saw the caller ID. "A friend from high school who I haven't heard from in years. Evidently the girls' identities have been released."

She let the phone ring without answering. Even if the phone hadn't needed to stay free for the kidnapper's call, she couldn't bear to go through the details again. Her friends would understand.

Adam shifted out of Reverse and headed toward the exit. "I'm hoping he was just trying to put your mother at ease."

"I guess. But the girls have been missing for hours now. We have to find them before dark. They've never spent the night away from me."

Hadley could feel herself sliding to the edge of hysteria. She took a deep breath, determined to stay in control. Losing it wouldn't help find the girls.

Adam turned to look at her. "Have you eaten anything today?"

"Not that I remember, but I'm not hungry. I doubt I could even swallow."

"You have to keep up your strength. Collapsing won't help anybody."

"I know. I'll try to eat something later. But if you're hungry we can stop somewhere."

"I can wait. I had breakfast."

He pulled out of the parking lot and into a stream of cars. "So is it back to the house?"

The empty, silent house void of Lila's laughter and Lacy's high-pitched chatter. No footsteps running down the long hallway no matter how many times she cautioned them to walk.

No one there to call "Momma."

"I don't think I can face going back there yet."

"Where would you like to go?"

"I don't know, but I can't just sit and do nothing while waiting on the kidnapper to call with a ransom request or the police to call with good news. The waiting is driving me insane."

"We can backtrack where the cops have been, search the nearby parks, go house to house and ask if anyone saw or heard anything last night."

"But that would only be reaching the same people who've already been questioned."

"What about going on television?" Adam suggested. "You can personally plead for the kidnapper to let them go or for someone to come forward with information."

"I like that." Hope spiked her pulse as the idea took hold. "Dallas has a big heart."

"It's the fastest way to reach hundreds of thousands of people," Adam agreed. "You can offer an award for information leading to the safe return of the girls. That might get a response from someone from the city's criminal element who actually knows the kidnapper."

"Or someone involved in the kidnapping," Hadley

said. "If we act now, I may be able to get on the evening news broadcast of every local TV channel."

"At least you should be able to make the ten o'clock news." Adam agreed.

"I'll call Detective Lane right now and see if he can set it up."

She grabbed her phone. Adam reached across the space between them and laid a hand on hers. "Just a suggestion, but if I were you, I think I'd bypass Lane with this and go directly to the local TV stations."

"Do you think the detective would have a problem with my decision?"

"I think he has his own way of handling things and might object," Adam said.

"If he has legitimate objections to my making a public plea, I'd like to hear them. I don't want to take any unnecessary risks where the girls' safety is concerned. I can't afford a dangerous mistake."

"I can't tell you what to do with this, Hadley. It's your daughters."

But not hers alone. "I'd appreciate your honest opinion," she said. "As a friend and as a male point of view."

Before he had time to answer, her cell phone rang again. This time it was a close friend who she hated to ignore. She took the call and accepted the empathy. Another call buzzed in.

Detective Lane. She told her friend a quick goodbye and took the detective's call. "Have you found Lacy and Lila?"

"Unfortunately, no."

Her spirit plunged. "What about the construction workers involved in the remodeling project? Did you check them out?"

"We're working on it, but at this point it doesn't appear that any of them have a criminal record."

Desperation forced her to ignore Adam's words of caution. She had to do something, and Lane could probably make the arrangements quicker than she could on her own.

"I want to go on television and plead for the girls' safe return," she said.

There was a long, silent pause before the detective responded. "We can discuss that possibility."

"I don't need to discuss the possibility. My mind's made up. The only question is will you help me arrange it or should I proceed on my own?"

"I'll set it up, Hadley, but we need to talk first. Do you mind if I call you Hadley?"

"Please do, and I'm not questioning your expertise or your methods, Detective. But unless you can assure me that you have a credible lead in finding Lacy and Lila, I insist we go forward with the TV spots immediately. There is no time to waste and no reason to talk about it."

"I agree, but we have a new development in the case."

She held her breath, a wave of dread rushing through her. If this was bad news… "What's the development?"

"Someone claiming to be the kidnapper has made contact."

Chapter Four

Hadley's heart was pounding as Adam pulled into her mother's driveway. At her frantic urging, Adam had broken the speed limit more than once on the way here.

Detective Lane had refused to give her any additional information on the phone except that there had been a ransom demand along with a promise by the kidnapper that Lacy and Lila were alive and well.

Alive.

The word echoed in her heart. But the detective's word choice continued to haunt her—someone *claiming* to be the kidnapper.

Please, God, let this be more than a claim.

She spotted the detective on the covered porch, standing in the stalking shadows cast by a pair of aged oak trees. She jumped from the truck as it rolled to a stop and raced to hear the rest of the story.

The detective was not smiling when he greeted her. She paused a few feet away as her gaze zeroed in on a FedEx envelope the detective held in his right hand along with a small plastic bag. When she looked closer she recognized the bag's contents.

A pink ribbon with a row of intricate hearts that she'd last seen tied around Lacy's ponytail.

She took a deep breath. "That's Lacy's ribbon. Where did you get it?"

"It came in the envelope with the message."

She gulped in air and relief. "Then the man isn't just claiming to be the kidnapper. He has my girls."

"You're sure about the ribbon."

"It looks exactly the same."

Only Hadley was certain Lacy's hair had not been in a ponytail when she'd gone to bed last night. The loose red curls had been spread about her pillow when Hadley tucked her in and kissed her good-night as well as when she'd checked on them just after one.

Now that she thought about it, Lacy's hair hadn't been in a ponytail when they'd taken her mother to the hospital. Lacy must have taken the ribbon out when she and Lila were playing dress-up with their grandmother's old hats, shawls and shoes just after lunch yesterday.

The kidnapper must have taken it from the dresser for this very purpose. "May I see the message?"

"Yes, but I think we should go inside and sit down first," the detective said.

"How much is the ransom demand?" she asked.

"Worry about that later," Adam said. "First, we should hear the detective out."

As if she had a choice. She fumbled in her purse for the house key before she remembered that Adam had locked up. He opened the door, and she led the way to the small formal living room where the detective had questioned her that morning.

Adam waited until she sat down and then dropped beside her on the sofa.

Adam Dalton, the man who had once thrilled her with his smile and made her blood run hot with his kisses. Adam, who had captured her heart so completely only to shatter it when it suited his purpose.

Letting him back into her life was likely the worst choice she could make for so many reasons. But this wasn't about her or protecting her heart or hiding her secrets.

Nothing mattered now except Lacy and Lila and bringing them safely home again.

Detective Lane took the chair directly across from Hadley and then took his time pulling a sheet of paper from the FedEx envelope. "This is only a copy," he said. "The actual note is considered evidence and is being checked for fingerprints and DNA residue."

The note was written in the type of scribbled print a first grader might produce. Hadley read it quickly before taking a deep breath and reading it a second time, this time out loud.

"Your daughters are safe and being well taken care of. If you want them to stay that way, do exactly as you're told from this point on. You have two days to get the ransom together. I want five million dollars delivered in unmarked twenty-dollar bills. Believe me, I will know if they're marked and you'll never see the twins again. Stay tuned for further instructions. Lacy and Lila send their love."

"Bastard." Adam followed that outburst with a string of muttered curses. He took the note and read it for himself before returning it to the detective. "Is that the envelope the note came in?"

"No, like the note, the original packaging has been taken as evidence. But the envelope was delivered at 5:32 this evening."

Hadley checked her watch. Just over an hour ago. "Was it delivered to the police station?"

"No. It was delivered here and addressed to you. The officer we had watching the house signed for it."

"I don't recall you mentioning this morning that officers were staking out the O'Sullivan home," Adam said.

"It's routine in a case like this." Lane reached across the coffee table and handed the plastic-encased ribbon to Hadley. "I need you to officially identify this without taking it out of the bag."

"It's Lacy's hair ribbon," Hadley said again. "But she wasn't wearing it when I tucked her into bed."

"When was the last time you saw the ribbon?"

"Yesterday afternoon, before we left for the hospital."

"You're sure?"

"Yes. I put her hair in a ponytail after lunch, but she must have taken it down when she and Lila were playing dress-up."

"So the ribbon might have been taken at any time yesterday afternoon?"

"Or taken when the girls were kidnapped." Adam shifted and sat straighter, meeting the detective's questioning stare head-on.

"Possibly," Lane agreed.

"How about just saying what you have to say, Detective, instead of playing games?" Adam said.

"The ransom note was dropped off at a downtown FedEx location at five minutes past nine last night," Lane said. "12:00 a.m. is the last pickup from that station for next-day delivery in the Dallas/Fort Worth area."

"That can't be right," Hadley said. "The girls were here and asleep at eleven after one. I checked on them myself."

"Maybe the clock you checked has the wrong time," Adam said.

"I don't think so," Hadley said. "But there's a quick

way to find out." She bolted to the bedroom with Adam and the detective at her heels.

The clock was to the minute with her watch. "I don't see how this could be," she said. "If the FedEx timing is accurate, it means the ribbon had to be taken and the ransom note written before the girls were abducted."

"Looks that way," Lane agreed.

Hadley wrapped her fingers around the bedpost. "There must be some mistake."

"Who mailed the note?" Adam asked.

"John Doe from a nonexistent address. The charges were paid with cash."

"So impossible to track," Adam said as they walked back to the small, formal living area. "That figures."

"But we do know the man will get in touch with us again," Hadley said. "He won't walk away from the chance to pick up five million dollars."

Five million dollars she didn't have and had little chance of coming up with on her own. Her mother lived well, but Hadley was almost certain she couldn't get her hands on that much money—not even if she sold the house. And selling the house would take far too much time.

"Is there some organization that lends money in abduction situations like this?" she asked.

"We'll deal with the ransom later," Lane said. "For now, let's concentrate on what we know. Someone had access to the house both before and at the time of the abduction. Apparently they come and go at will. That significantly narrows down our suspects."

He put up his hand and counted off on his fingers. "Your mother. You. Am I missing anyone?"

"Matilda," Hadley said, knowing exactly whom he was referring to.

Lane crossed an ankle over the opposite knee. "Do you know that she has a younger brother with a criminal record?"

"Quinton."

"So you do know him?"

"I know his first name and that he exists. I didn't know he had a criminal record."

"His last name is Larson," Lane said. "Exactly what do you know about him?"

"Not much. He's a quite a bit younger than Matilda."

"Have you ever met him?"

"I have. Years ago, Mother occasionally hired him when she needed something done that was too strenuous for Matilda. I think he may have been living with Matilda's family at the time. Her husband was still alive then."

"What kind of tasks did he do for your mother?"

"Whatever she needed done that didn't require a professional. Moving heavy furniture, washing windows, cleaning out the garage. But he hasn't worked here in years, actually not since my fourteenth birthday when my mother ordered him off the property. I'm twenty-nine now."

"But you no longer live in the area, so you can't be sure she hasn't hired him for similar tasks lately?"

"I seriously doubt that. Mother is very generous, but she is not one to forgive and forget. Besides, she hires Matilda's son, Sam, to help out now. Mother likes him a lot. Says he's polite and dependable.

"And she hires Matilda's daughter when she entertains. I've even used Alana to babysit on a few occasions. The girls love her."

Adam shifted so that he faced her. "What did Quinton do to upset her?"

It had been a long time ago. Hadley had put the ex-

perience behind her and moved on years ago. Yet the
disturbing memories came flooding back now.

"Quinton and I were in the kitchen. He was on a step-
stool, taking down Mother's crystal serving trays. When
I started making a sandwich, he asked me to make him
one, too. I said sure. While I worked on that, he came
over and started teasing me about my birthday. He said I
was old enough to have some real fun now. Probably not
his exact words, but that was the gist of the taunting."

"How old was Quinton at the time?" Lane asked.

"I'm not sure. Around eighteen, I think. He'd been
expelled from high school for the year. I never knew
why."

"Is teasing as far as it went?" Adam asked.

"No. When I started to leave, he grabbed my arm and
pulled me back into the kitchen. He started touching my
breasts. I told him to stop. He just laughed."

Lane took a pen and pad from his shirt pocket.
"Where was your mother and Matilda when this happened?"

"Outside, hanging party decorations. I was about to
yell for them when Quinton reached under by skirt. I
picked up the handiest weapon I saw and hit him over
the head with it. It turned out to be Mother's favorite
and most expensive vase. She'd set it out to use for a
centerpiece that night."

"Guess that got Quinton's attention," Lane said.

"It got everyone's attention. The vase hit the floor
and broke into a thousand shards. Quinton started yelling and cursing at the top of his lungs, and he was bleed-
ing. I figured I'd be in big trouble."

"Surely you weren't," Adam said. "He got what he
deserved."

"Exactly what Mother said when I told her what had

happened. She exploded. So did Matilda, but all the ire was directed at Quinton. Mother ordered him out of the house. I never saw him again."

"Evidently, you didn't hit him hard enough," Lane said. "He didn't change his ways."

"What kind of crimes has he been charged with?" Adam asked.

"Cashing bad checks, burglary, but mostly domestic abuse. Guy has a mean temper and no respect for women. Practically killed one of his live-ins when he cracked her skull with a frying pan for swiping some of his crack cocaine."

"Sounds like a real sweetheart," Adam said.

Hadley's blood ran cold at the thought of her girls being in his hands. "Surely he's in jail."

"You'd think," Lane agreed. "But no. The girlfriend decided to forgive him and dropped charges. He has done some jail time for other infractions, but thanks to a lenient judge, he's out on parole at the moment."

Adam stood and started to pace. "Have you questioned him?"

"We will, as soon as we locate him."

"Isn't staying in the area a condition of his parole?" Adam asked.

"Career criminals who keep getting off with light sentences don't tend to take parole too seriously. But we'll find him."

"Did Matilda tell you about Quinton?" Hadley asked.

"No, and neither did your mother, or you, for that matter."

"I haven't seen him in fifteen years. His name didn't come to mind."

Hadley's mind drifted from the conversation to the chances that Matilda might know how to find her brother. If she did, would she tell the detective or would she consider family loyalty more important? The former, Hadley decided, especially if there was even a chance he had Lacy and Lila.

She tuned back to the current conversation when she saw Adam bristle and heard the change in his tone.

"I don't like where this is going, Detective."

"You don't get to call the shots, Adam."

"That's why Hadley should get an attorney."

"Why is it I need an attorney?"

"The good detective just insinuated you might be more than the victim."

She shouldn't have let her mind wander for even a second. "What are you talking about?"

"I was merely stating the facts," the detective said.

"Save your breath," Adam said. "The fact is that Hadley had nothing to do with the abduction."

"I didn't say that she did. I only remarked that being a single mother of two children can get very difficult. The stress has been known to push some mothers over the edge."

Hadley stared at the detective as his words sank in. "Are you actually suggesting that I might be involved in Lacy and Lila's disappearance?"

"I'm just saying it's been known to happen."

She jumped up, her hands flying to her hips. "No, what you're suggesting is that I got rid of my daughters to make life easier on myself. I know monsters have done that before, but I'm not a monster. I may be insane with worry, but I'm not insane."

"I'm glad to hear that." Lane's expression didn't back that up. Nor did he look convinced.

Her anger raged. "Are you even looking for my daughters or are you and your fellow cops just sitting around trying to think of ways to trap me into admitting guilt?"

"You're way off base and you know it."

"Do I?" Her insides churned so violently, she grew dizzy. "Get out, Detective."

"I'm going," Lane said. "I'll come back when we have something new or when you calm down enough to talk rationally. In the meantime, don't leave the area."

"I'm not going anywhere without my daughters."

She didn't walk the detective to the door, but when she heard it close behind him, she turned to Adam. "Do you think I'm a depraved monster, too?"

"Not for a second." He stood, walked to her side and pulled her shaking body into his arms.

That was all it took. Her tears broke loose like floodwaters. This time she didn't try to hold them back.

She clung to Adam and let the pain and desperation spill onto his broad shoulders. Right or wrong, he was all she had to hold on to now.

ADAM'S HEAD RESTED atop the soft swirls of Hadley's silky hair as her hot tears soaked his shirt. The bitterness and resentment toward her he'd nursed through his own dark days fell away like ashes from a smoldering log.

In spite of the seriousness of the situation, he couldn't stop the memories from creeping back into his mind. The pain of the last time he'd held her in his arms hit the hardest.

She'd been crying that night, too, afraid for him, terrified that he might come home from the war in a coffin. He'd comforted her that night with kisses and passion and vows of forever.

All in the past. He had to let it go.

Still, it was killing him to watch her endure this. Her fear for her daughters was palpable, and with every tick of the clock the danger became more menacing, the tension more intense.

Shelton Lane's insensitive comments definitely hadn't helped. Adam had been sorely tempted to plant a fist in the man's face. Thankfully, he'd managed to hold back. Going to jail for assaulting an officer would have left Hadley to spend the night in this house all alone.

Instead, she was in his arms.

But she needed a hell of a lot more than a shoulder to cry on. She needed a hero. So did Lacy and Lila. His mother had thought he could be that man, but there were so many missing pieces to the puzzle he didn't know where to begin.

Hadley sniffled and pulled away. "I'm sorry, Adam. I didn't mean to lose control like that. I hate being weak."

"You're anything but weak, Hadley."

She pressed the palms of her hands against his wet shirt. "You're soaked."

"The shirt will dry. It's fine. How about some food?" he asked, changing the subject.

"I'm not hungry, but you can check the fridge. There are likely fixings for a sandwich or a salad, but probably little else unless you like yogurt, raw veggies or fruit. Mother's on a health kick."

"I'm sure I can wrangle up something."

"Make yourself at home. I need to call Mother and tell her that we heard from the kidnapper and that he's promised the girls are safe. That may let her get a little bit of much-needed rest tonight."

"You might want to give yourself a few minutes to think things through concerning Matilda's brother before you call."

"I'll just tell Mother what the detective told us. I'm sure it hasn't occurred to her that Quinton could be involved. If it had, she would have given his name to Detective Lane."

"Will you call Matilda?"

"I won't have to. Mother will have her on the phone in seconds after we hang up to see if she knows how to find Quinton."

"I imagine someone with the DPD has already done that. For the record, I'm sure they're checking me out, as well."

"I'm sorry, but I'm sure you'll pass muster with flying colors."

"Unless they think a few speeding tickets make me a risk."

But they would question his and Hadley's relationship.

"Go ahead and call your mom," he urged. "I'll check out the fridge."

Hadley followed him into the kitchen but went straight for a cup of stale, black coffee. He inspected the food options and decided on turkey sausage, eggs and toast. Hopefully, he could convince Hadley to try a few bites.

He got started on the sausage while Hadley made the call. Her voice remained surprisingly steady as she inquired about how her mother was feeling and then quickly described the contents and delivery details of the FedEx package.

It was obvious when the topic switched to him.

"Yes, he's still here, Mother." Pause. "Because I asked him to stay." Another pause. "That's my decision."

Adam could understand Janice not being thrilled to

have him back in the picture, but you'd think he'd be preferable to having Hadley face this alone.

Once again, he wondered where in the hell the girls' father was and why he hadn't come up again in tonight's discussion with the detective. Whatever Hadley had told the detective about him this morning must have been enough to take him completely out of the picture.

"Can you just please let it go for now, Mother? There's something far more urgent we need to talk about. I'm switching to speaker now so that Adam can join in the conversation."

"I have nothing to say to Adam."

Janice O'Sullivan's voice came through loud and clear.

"Then just listen for a minute. Based on what we know now, whoever took the girls had to have easy access to the house," Hadley said. "Both day and night."

"You know I would have changed every lock on every door and window if I'd any idea the girls were in danger."

"I know and I'm not blaming you for a second."

"The locks were all changed when we did the remodeling," Janice said. "That's only been a few months ago, I'm certain there aren't a lot of working keys floating around."

"You didn't mention that earlier."

"I just remembered it. I think it's the pain meds. They keep me groggy. I told them I'm leaving the hospital in the morning. You need me and they can't keep me against my will."

"I need you to do what the doctor tells you to do, but I'm glad you remembered changing the locks. That narrows the suspect list down even further."

"It doesn't matter who took them," Janice said.

"When he shows up to collect the ransom, the police can arrest him. I saw them do that on television just the other night."

"The police are considering all options," Hadley assured her. "Detective Lane brought up the name of Quinton Larson."

"Matilda's brother?"

"Yes. Did you know he has a criminal record?"

"I know Matilda was always bailing him out of trouble, but I can't see what that has to do with anything now."

"It's possible that he got hold of Matilda's keys and had an extra set made."

"Not any time lately."

"How can you be so sure?"

"Quinton Larson has been dead for at least five years."

"You must have him confused with someone else."

"Not hardly. I paid for his funeral."

Hadley dropped to a kitchen chair as if that bombshell had knocked her legs out from under her.

Adam sat down beside her. "And you're sure the funeral was for Quinton and not one of Matilda's other brothers?" he questioned.

"Matilda didn't have any other brothers. It was just her and Quinton. That's why she felt responsible for him after her mother died. Why all of this interest in Quinton?"

"Detective Lane checked him out as a person of interest," Hadley said. "According to him, Quinton Larson is not only alive but out of jail on probation."

"The detective is confused. There may be a Quinton Larson out on probation, but it's not Matilda's brother," Janice insisted. "I'll call Matilda right now to prove it."

"Good idea, Mom. Call me back after you've talked to her."

Adam fell to his own thoughts, barely listening to the rest of the conversation. If Detective Lane did have the right man, Matilda's brother was a perverted, violent son of a bitch who he wouldn't trust with a rabid wolf much less two young, innocent girls.

And had Matilda Bastion been half as trustworthy as Hadley and her mother believed, she'd have never conned Janice into paying for a funeral for a man who was not only breathing but out beating up women.

Adam cracked a few eggs and beat them with a vengeance. If Detective Lane didn't find Quinton by morning, he would. Or at least he'd give it his best shot—inside and outside the law.

No way he could sit back and do nothing while Hadley's daughters were in the hands of a man devoid of morals. A madman playing games with Hadley's mind with his taunting.

Ransom note or not, Adam didn't trust him to keep the girls safe or alive.

MARY NELL FINGERED the wiry hair of the doll that Lila held clutched to her chest. "Look how cute they look all snuggled up in the bed together and sound asleep," she whispered.

"Five million dollars worth of cute."

She moved away from the bed. "When do we get the money? I can't wait to be rich."

"As soon as I get all the details for getting out of the country worked out."

"Maybe we could go to Paris to live. I always wanted to see that Eiffel Tower."

"Forget that. I'm not going to no friggin' France. Besides we'd lose too much money when we exchanged our good old American dollars for euros."

"I could go topless on one of them Riviera beaches."

"You can go topless anywhere we end up, baby, anytime I say."

"I wish you'd stay with me and the girls tonight."

"You know I can't do that. I gotta be present and accounted for when the cops come calling."

"So what do I do if the cops show up here?"

"They won't. But don't get too attached to those red-headed brats. They get me a ticket to freedom or they get to fly around with the angels. They ain't staying with me."

"You mean with *us?*"

"Sure, baby. You know I wouldn't leave you stranded."

He pinched her nipples hard, ran his tongue down her throat and left. It seemed she was taking all the risks. But it was better this way. She'd take care of the girls—no matter what.

Five million dollars. That would take them anywhere they wanted to go. The good life was practically theirs.

WEARINESS NOT ONLY weighed heavy on Shelton Lane's shoulders, it seemed to settle in his bones. Worse, a dull ache was attacking at the base of his skull.

It was always like this when a child went missing. The pressure never let up. He'd seen too many of the cases turn out bad. That kind of thing stayed with a cop all his life.

Sometimes you knew going in that the chance of a happy ending was slim to none. Most time you didn't. But you always knew time was of the essence.

This case really had him puzzled. Hadley O'Sullivan had been on the edge of complete hysteria when he'd arrived this morning. He hadn't figured that for an act. But the evidence all pointed to the fact that this was some kind of inside job, especially the ransom note sent even before the abduction took place.

Looked to him like it was sent just to throw off the cops and make them think the crime was about money. He wouldn't be shocked if that was the last message they received from the kidnapper.

Which left Hadley O'Sullivan as the one with the most likely motive and plenty of opportunity and means. If the girls were out of the picture, she could go on with her life unencumbered with lover Adam Dalton.

Shelton definitely didn't buy the friend story. All he had to do was look at them together to know that there was more going on between them than that. The guy might be a tough-as-nails former marine, but he had his heart on his sleeve where Hadley was concerned.

Shelton turned onto the I-20 entrance ramp. He'd love to go home and crash in his bed. But even if he fell asleep, it wouldn't stick more than a few minutes. The first twenty-four hours of an abduction case were the most urgent. This one was going on sixteen hours now.

When he reached the station, he grabbed a cup of black coffee and went straight to his desk. He shuffled through his messages. The one he wanted was about halfway through the pile, attached to a research file he'd ordered on Hadley O'Sullivan.

The note at the top said it all.

Hadley O'Sullivan had been caught in a blatant lie.

Chapter Five

Adam woke abruptly, his senses keen, his instincts sharp. That had been the means of survival in Afghanistan when he'd learned to sleep in short spurts and wake up ready to spring into action.

Back then his body was up to the task. The bullets and the burns he'd suffered when their patrol had been ambushed put a quietus on that. Even after two years of rehab, he didn't have the raw strength or the agility he'd once taken for granted.

He stretched and sat up on the couch slowly, trying to overcome the stiffness that had settled into his muscles and joints.

Oddly thoughts of R.J. crept into his mind. Yesterday morning at this time he'd been dreading his trip to the Dry Gulch Ranch for the reading of the will.

But R.J. wasn't dead. He'd decided years too late he wanted a chance at being a father. But where was Lila and Lacy's father. Had he opted out of their lives? Or was he somehow involved in the abduction? And why was Hadley so determined to keep everything about him a secret?

Aches persisted as Adam stood and went in search of Hadley. He found her lying sideways across one of the twin beds in the room where she'd put her daughters to bed two nights ago.

Like him, she was fully clothed except for the sandals she'd kicked out of and left next to the bed. Even in sleep, she looked tormented. He doubted she'd slept an hour, though the first light of dawn crept into the room through the slatted blinds.

She'd paced most of the night, jumped every time her phone rang and then ignored the call when a friend's name popped up on the caller ID screen.

Moving as silently as he could, Adam grabbed the lightweight quilt from the other bed and spread it across her bare feet and legs.

He started to walk away, but poignant images from their past stole into his mind. Nights when he'd slept beside her, their bodies entangled, still slick from their lovemaking. Who'd have ever thought they would end up like this? Together but yet worlds apart.

And he would never make love to her again. That might be the cruelest trick the war had played on him. Doctors had given him back his life but not his manhood.

One day, he might be able to examine the past with a degree of objectivity. But not now. The stakes were too high to get bogged down in what-ifs.

Getting Lila and Lacy back safely wasn't only the top priority. It had to be the only priority.

Tiptoeing from the room, Adam walked to the kitchen, emptied the stale coffee and old grounds and started a fresh pot. The sound of hammering broke the early-morning silence.

Raking his fingers through his thick, mussed hair, he went toward the front lawn to check it out. He spotted two middle-aged women in jogging suits about halfway between him and the curb. One steadied a yard sign. The other pounded the stake that would anchor it in place.

"What's with the racket? It's barely dawn."

The woman kept hammering.

"This is private property," he called as he started walking in their direction. His socks became wet with dew as he hurried across the manicured grass.

The woman with the hammer waved it at him threateningly. "We don't want murdering mothers in our neighborhood." She stood back so that he got a good look at the sign.

CHILD KILLER

The words were printed in bright red spray paint that dripped from the letters like fresh blood.

Fury gripped him, bunching his muscles, knotting in his stomach. He rushed toward them and yanked the sign from the ground.

"Hadley O'Sullivan is going through hell right now. She hasn't slept, hasn't eaten, can barely breathe she's so worried about her daughters."

"Not according to what I read in the paper."

"Get off this property *now*."

One woman backed away a few steps. The other held on to the hammer and stood her ground. "If you're here with her, you're probably as guilty as she is. You'll both burn in hell."

There was no reasoning with her and Adam was in no mood to bother. "Set foot on this property again and I'll have you and any other lunatics you bring with you arrested. Is that clear?"

"Don't threaten me."

"If you're not gone in five seconds, the threat becomes reality. One. Two."

Both women retreated to the curb. A passing car

slowed to a crawl. Someone in the passenger side rolled down the window and stuck out a camera with a large telephoto lens. Adam resisted the urge to give a fitting one-finger salute.

The two women finally climbed into their station wagon and drove away, taking their sign and hammer with them. Adam picked up the morning paper and plodded back inside. Hopefully he'd seen the end of the two misinformed vigilantes, but he wouldn't count on it. Even misdirected rage had a way of inciting more hatred.

He went to the kitchen, poured a cup of coffee and sat down to skim the morning's headlines. His eyes zeroed in on an article at the bottom of the first page.

No Sign of Break-in at Home of Missing Twin Girls

That explained the sign.

He read the article. While it didn't directly label Hadley a suspect in the twins' disappearance, it definitely leaned in that direction.

"Is that this morning's paper?"

He looked up. Hadley was standing in the doorway, her hair disheveled, her slacks and cotton shirt wrinkled and in disarray. There were dark shadows beneath her red-rimmed green eyes.

"Today's *Dallas Morning News,*" he said, wishing he could shield her from the disturbing article, but knowing it wouldn't help. If he didn't show it to her, she'd hear about it from someone else.

"Sit down and I'll get you some coffee," he offered.

"Thanks. Did you get any sleep at all last night?"

"Very little. The same as you."

"I'll sleep when the girls are home again."

Adam sat a mug of coffee next to her elbow. "Drink this and then I'll make you some breakfast."

"Didn't I just force down a meal?"

"More like a couple of bites and that was hours ago."

She took a few sips of coffee and then slid the newspaper over so that she could see the front page. Her expression grew pained as she read. As exhausted as she was, she understood that the bizarre facts surrounding the case were making her look guilty. At least now, she might consider getting an attorney.

Adam doubted if even that would be enough if this dragged on much longer.

If he were going to make any kind of stab at being a hero, it was time to act.

HADLEY DIDN'T NOTICE the hot coffee sloshing from her mug until Adam rushed forward with a paper towel to dab it from her arm.

"Did you get burned?"

"If I did, I'm too irritated to notice. This article deliberately makes it look as if what actually happened is too preposterous to be true."

"Ignore it. You know reporters like to spice up a story."

"Detective Lane is not a reporter and he also insinuated last night that I'm somehow implicated in everything that's happened."

"I don't think he believes you're guilty for a minute. Anyone can see how upset you are. He's just doing his job and that means investigating this from every angle."

"It's his job to get my daughters back. They know all about me and Mom and even the housekeeper. They can't even locate Quinton Larson, and this man who hasn't been around this house in over a decade seems to be the only lead they have."

"At least the only lead they've shared with us. They

have more," Adam reminded her. "They may have Quinton in custody by now."

"If the Quinton they're talking about is even Matilda's supposedly dead brother. And they don't have Lacy and Lila or we would have heard. We don't even have a plan for what to do about the ransom. I can't snap my fingers and have five million dollars drop from the sky."

"All good points," Adam agreed. "So maybe we should look at this from a new angle."

"Why not? Do you have one?"

"I have a good marine buddy whose brother is one of the top hostage negotiators in the world."

"This isn't a hostage situation."

"It's not your *typical* hostage situation, but the kidnapper is holding the girls hostage. Besides, Chuck Casey's brother was involved in at least one famous child abduction case."

"What case was that?"

"Three years ago the son of a Houston shipping tycoon was taken from his private school following an after-school football game."

"I remember that case," Hadley said. "Wasn't it a former chauffeur who abducted the kid?"

"Yes, and according to Chuck, his brother Fred is the main reason the family had a happy ending. I'm not sure Fred is available or even in the country, but we can ask."

"Call your friend," she said. This might be exactly the break they needed. Except... "Let Fred Casey know up front that I don't want any risky heroics. I won't take chances with my daughters' lives."

"I'll make sure he knows that."

"Perfect. I'll get showered and dressed while you try to get in touch with him. I need to check on Mother in person and find out if she ever got in touch with Matilda."

The last time Hadley had checked in with her mother and her private nurse had been at ten after nine last night. Her mother had left messages for Matilda to call her back but hadn't heard from her. The nurse had suggested Hadley not call again until morning. She had just given Janice an injection to control the pain and felt her patient needed to rest undisturbed.

Adam dropped a couple of pieces of wheat bread into the toaster. "It could be that Matilda was dodging Janice's calls."

"I find that difficult to believe. But if she is, I'll pay a call to Matilda and confront her about Quinton myself."

"Mind if I tag along?"

Oddly, she'd just assumed that he would. In a matter of hours, she'd let him back in her life—an act that would have been unthinkable before.

Desperation had changed all the rules.

"You can come, but don't expect a warm greeting or any thanks from Mother."

"I won't. That same warning might go for you when you call on Matilda."

Hadley sincerely hoped he was wrong about that. But if Quinton wasn't dead, and Matilda had conned Janice out of money for his funeral, then Hadley didn't know Matilda at all.

"You'll have to live with the whiskers until I get my hands on a razor, but if it's okay with you, I'll just throw what I'm wearing into the washing machine, dry it and wear it again," Adam said. "That won't take long and I'll smell a lot better."

"No problem. The downstairs laundry room is just past the walk-through pantry."

Hadley pointed in the right direction. She could have offered him her razor, but for some weird reason she liked the edgy look of his whiskered chin. It fit better with her ragged appearance.

He grabbed the toast from the toaster and set one on a saucer. "Munch on that with your coffee," he said. He took the other with him as he left.

Hadley stood and walked to the kitchen window. Her gaze fastened on the gingerbread-style playhouse her mother had gotten her handyman to build for the girls. They'd clapped their hands and started yelling when they saw it for the first time.

Lila had smelled the miniature pot of petunias and then peeked through the curtained windows, her eyes wide with wonder. Impetuous Lacy had opened the bright pink door and rushed inside.

Furnished with a child-size table and chairs, non-working refrigerator and range and a shelf full of plastic dishes and cooking paraphernalia, it was every little girl's dream.

"You'll play in it again," she whispered to no one. "You're coming home."

She had to hang on to that hope or she'd never make it through the day. Already her body felt as if it had been used for a punching bag. The fear for Lacy and Lila was eating away at her like acid, corroding her nerves and brain and sucking her energy.

She was still staring out the window minutes later when Adam reappeared wearing one of her mother's robes, his dirty clothes in hand. Even in pink silk, he looked virile, a man's man. Tough but not arrogant or chauvinistic. That had been one of the first qualities that had attracted her to him.

"Chuck got hold of Fred and explained the situation to him. He said to count him in."

"Is he in Texas?"

"He's in D.C. now, but he'll catch the first available flight to Dallas. He said he'll call when he gets to town. He said to assure you that he never takes unnecessary risks with lives, but he also has a couple of requirements before he'll agree to get involved."

"Which are?"

"He expects complete honesty from you about every detail. He wants no surprises about the facts."

"What else?"

"He needs you to trust him completely. Second-guessing him and veering from the plan will jeopardize the girls' safety."

Complete trust would mean everything was out of her hands. She took a deep breath and exhaled slowly. "I'm not sure I can promise that."

"Then trust in me, Hadley. If I think Fred is making a mistake, I'll step in and either take over or find someone who can. Someone who believes in you fully and doesn't have to play by the rules."

Trust Adam. She had once. He'd betrayed her. But this was different. This was about his abilities as a decision-maker and his hero qualities. They had never been in question.

"Okay, Adam. Tell Fred the girls are in his hands." Now, if the kidnapper would just call back and give them a place and a time and five million dollars would fall like manna from heaven.

A lesser miracle would do just fine, too. As long as it brought Lacy and Lila home.

In the meantime, she'd call Detective Lane for an update. It had been almost twenty-four hours since she'd discovered their empty beds.

MATILDA'S SANDALS CLICKED against the concrete steps of the church. She'd slipped out of the Thursday morning mass early, not wanting to leave with the others and face the questions of friends and acquaintances. They'd all want to know about little Lacy and Lila and she was too upset to talk about the kidnapping.

She was frightened for herself as well as the girls. Keys to Janice O'Sullivan's house had gone missing from her key ring sometime since Monday morning. That was the last time she remembered using a key to Janice's house. When Janice was home, Matilda always rang the bell and Janice would let her in.

She hadn't realized they were missing until the morning the girls had gone missing. If they turned up in the hands of the kidnapper, she could be in real trouble. Officer Grummet had made it clear from his questioning that he already thought she might be involved in the crime.

And now Janice had left a message asking about Quinton. Matilda had no choice but to tell her the truth. That would cost Matilda her job. That was no one's fault but her own. Lying always led to more lies. The end result was never good.

Matilda should have never let Quinton back into her life. He'd talked a great story of redemption when he'd called last week and begged her to see him. He'd convinced her he'd finally found religion and turned his life around.

She probably hadn't been that hard to convince. She'd prayed for it for so long. He was her only brother. She loved him. And she owed him. He'd saved her life more than once when their daddy had staggered home drunk and had come at her.

But if Quinton was behind this abduction, if he hurt those precious little girls, she'd turn him in to the cops herself without blinking an eye.

Quinton hadn't stayed long when he'd dropped by Monday afternoon. They'd sipped iced tea at the kitchen table and he'd asked about Sam and Alana who were both out at the time. When he'd asked about her job, she'd told him about Janice's upcoming operation.

Another major mistake. He might have gotten the idea right then and there to rob her house while she was in the hospital. Then when he'd discovered that Hadley and the girls were staying there, he'd decided to go for real money.

Those were only assumptions, but they would explain everything.

Admittedly, Quinton hadn't had much of a chance to steal the keys to Janice's house. The only time he'd been alone was the few minutes it had taken her to go to the bathroom and then to the bedroom to get the hundred dollars she'd lent him.

But the keys were in plain sight, on the hook in the kitchen where she always kept them. He could have tried the keys on her doors in a matter of seconds and known which ones didn't fit. By the process of simple elimination he'd have realized the other two house keys were to the O'Sullivan home.

It pained her to think that Quinton could commit such a depraved and heartless act. But if he hadn't taken the keys, where were they?

She whirled around at the sound of footsteps behind her. "Johnny. What are you doing here?"

"Looking for you. I figured you'd be at mass praying for the O'Sullivan girls."

"You know me well."

Far better than most mechanics knew their customers. Quinton had worked for Johnny Rouse years ago, before Johnny had fired him for stealing from the cash register. But she had kept taking her cars to Johnny for repairs. They'd started dating a couple of years ago after his wife left him.

"Do the police have any leads?" Johnny asked.

"None that I've been told about."

"Hadley's gotta be really upset. Her mother, too."

"They are. We all are."

"Hopefully they'll find them today."

"And find them alive and safe," Matilda added.

She started walking again. Johnny kept pace.

"I heard you came by the shop yesterday looking for me," he said.

"I did."

"My workers said you were acting crazy. Said you insisted they waste an hour looking for some stupid keys."

"I thought I might have lost them when I brought my car in for an oil change Tuesday afternoon."

"You had to have your keys when you left, Matilda, or you couldn't have driven your car home."

"I lost house keys, not car keys."

"Well, I didn't see no loose keys of any kind lying about the shop after you left. I s'pect they'll show up around your house in a day or two."

"I s'pect so," she agreed. "But keep an eye out for them, will you? If you find them, please call me."

"Sure."

In spite of Johnny's prediction, there was an extremely slim chance they'd show up at her house.

There wasn't a square inch of space she hadn't already searched.

But they could be at Janice's house. The problem was she couldn't get into the house unless Hadley was there. And she couldn't very well turn the house upside down searching for the keys if Hadley was there without admitting she'd lost them.

She would admit it, if it came to that. She hoped it wouldn't. She couldn't afford a lawyer. And what would Alana and Sam do if she went to jail and couldn't work and pay the bills?

"I guess you know Sam stopped in yesterday after you left."

"He didn't mention it to me."

"Yeah, he asked me about a job."

"What did you tell him?"

"I didn't. By the time I finished what I was doing and had time to talk to him about it, he'd gone."

"He's not very motivated. Having to go to summer school when he thought he'd be graduated by now has really bummed him out."

"Kids. Say, you wanna grab a bite to eat and catch a movie Saturday night? There's a new James Bond flick out."

"Another time, Johnny. I'm not really up to watching a movie."

"You might be if those girls are safe and sound. I'll keep in touch."

"Okay."

He took her hand and squeezed it. "You take care, Matilda."

"I will."

Johnny was a good guy. He liked her a lot but it was clear he wanted more than friendship. He wasn't a bad catch. He owned his own mechanic shop. He didn't curse much and when they went out he never drank more than a few beers.

Only problem was she'd had true love before with her husband. She knew how great it could be. She didn't love Johnny.

Her cell phone rang. It was Janice again. She couldn't dodge her forever, but she didn't want to explain her lies over the phone, especially not when Janice was recovering from surgery and in such horrifying angst about her granddaughters.

She wanted to talk to Janice face-to-face. It was the Christian thing to do.

Officer Grummet she could do without.

ADAM COULDN'T WAIT to sit down with Fred Casey and come up with a plan of action for dealing with the kidnapper. He'd had a fairly lengthy conversation with him while Fred was waiting at the Dulles Airport and Adam's clothes tumbled in the dryer. The man's knowledge and expertise were impressive.

He'd shared with Fred the latest information Hadley had received from Detective Lane. There had been several reported sightings of Lacy and Lila. They were all being checked out, but Lane wasn't convinced that any of them were credible at this point.

The police had not, as yet, located Quinton Larson, but they had reason to believe he was in the North Texas area.

Lacy's and Lila's pictures had gone out to every police agency in the country. Local police were currently making house calls on every child sex offender in the city. Apparently there were many.

Adam considered all the information as he dressed

in jeans and a shirt still warm from the dryer. He had one shoe on when he heard the screech of brakes in front of the house.

He hobbled to the door. Hadley beat him to it. She opened it and an instant attack of flashbulbs left them both blinking and squinting.

When he could see again, he noted that the van in the driveway was unmarked, evidence they weren't from one of the major local TV channels. They'd no doubt be next.

"Who are you and what do you want?" Hadley demanded.

"We're from a national magazine and we'd like to help you get out the facts about your daughters' kidnapping."

"Ms. O'Sullivan is not doing any interviews," Adam announced.

"Just a few questions," a perky blonde with a microphone insisted. "Where is the father of your missing daughters?"

Adam would have liked to hear the answer to that himself. Instead he stepped in front of Hadley, sheltering her from the push of the reporter and cameramen. "Ms. O'Sullivan has no comment except that her daughters, Lacy and Lila, are missing and her only concern is their safe return."

"Who are you?"

None of their damn business. "A longtime friend." He forced the door shut.

"I wasn't prepared for that," Hadley admitted. "I felt like I was about to be mauled by a pack of wolves."

"It will likely get a lot worse."

"Then perhaps I should have answered their questions so they'd go away and not come back."

"They'll only be replaced by a new wolf pack."

"So I'm forced to deal with vultures every time I open my door."

Adam had a thousand reservations about what he was about to suggest. He couldn't imagine how the idea had popped into his head. "I know a place that would make it a lot more difficult for the media wolf pack to get in your face."

"Jail?"

"A little more comfortable than that."

"What's to keep them back?"

"Barbed wire. Possibly a few riled bulls. Fear of getting shot by a cantankerous old man."

"And where would I find all of this?"

"At the Dry Gulch Ranch, home of the worst father I never had."

Chapter Six

Hadley's world was in a tailspin. Adam was an apparition who'd moved into the nightmare and taken control. She wasn't complaining. She wasn't sure how she'd get through this without him. As it was, she was holding on to sanity by a thread.

With the girls missing, the reasons she'd had for avoiding all contact with him had become meaningless. Every priority in her life had shifted or disappeared altogether.

Every priority except Lila and Lacy. Her life had centered on them from the moment she'd first held them in her arms. She'd give her life to keep them safe.

Only now it was others she had to depend on to do that for her. Detective Shelton Lane, whom she didn't fully trust and who didn't fully trust her. A hostage negotiator she'd never met. Adam Dalton, the man she'd vowed never to rely on again.

And now the father Adam had never mentioned before and whom he admittedly had no emotional attachment to had been added to the list.

Hadley tossed some underwear into an overnight bag. "Tell me more about R.J. What's his story and claim to fame?"

"Which version do you want?"

"How many versions are there?"

"There's my mother's. She says he's a gambling, heavy-drinking womanizer with no redeeming qualities. She divorced him when I was four."

"Smart woman." Hadley added two pairs of shorts to the suitcase. "Do you remember him at all from when you were a kid?"

"Very little. I remember riding with him on a gigantic horse, but then I suspect all horses are gigantic when you're that young. R.J. is still into horses and owns several thoroughbreds. Which reminds me, you may want to take a pair of jeans and some boots with you. This is a working ranch of sorts."

"I don't plan to be there long enough to rope and brand."

"Just saying, it's a rustic environment."

She took a pair of jeans from her closet. "Any other memories of R.J.?"

"I have a vague recollection of his holding me as we swung by a rope and dropped into the water."

"Was that a frightening memory?"

"Evidently not. I still love grabbing hold of a gnarly rope, swinging out over an old Texas swimming hole and dropping into a pool of splashing water."

"When I met you, you never even mentioned your biological father. When did the two of you reconnect?"

"We haven't."

"Don't tell me we're just going to drop in on a gambling drunk you haven't seen since you were four?"

"I've seen him once. We didn't work on bridging the disconnect."

"When was that?"

"Yesterday. In fact, I was there for the reading of his will when I heard about the kidnapping."

She added a pair of red cowboy boots and then zipped her bag while she tried to make sense of that last statement.

"Okay, Adam. Simplify. Is R.J. dead or alive?"

"He's alive—for now—and reportedly ready to get reacquainted with his offspring. He's about to get that chance with me."

Adam picked up her luggage and started toward the door.

"At least call and tell him we're coming."

"Why? If he didn't like surprises, he wouldn't have shown up for the reading of his own ridiculous will."

The sound of engines and skidding tires gave warning that the next round of media shots were about to fire.

"Let's get out of here while we still can," Adam said. "I'll explain what little else I know about R.J. on the way to the hospital."

"If we can get out," she said, fearing they were blocked in.

"We'll get out," Adam assured her.

He proved it with some forceful maneuvering to push through reporters and cameramen from a local TV station. Once in the truck, he started the engine and lay on the horn, sending the wolf pack scattering.

One of the vans didn't move. Adam went around them, taking out one of her mother's prized flower beds and leaving deep ruts in the lawn.

Hadley didn't notice the sign until they were backing past it.

CHILD KILLER

Printed in what looked like dripping blood. Her insides recoiled violently.

"They're *not* dead. Lacy and Lila are alive. Why would anyone say such a thing?"

Adam reached over and gave her hand a quick squeeze as he gunned the engine and left the hideous sign behind. "Pay no attention. It was put there by a couple of women with a twisted sense of justice."

"How do you know that?"

"Because I ran them off at daybreak. Should have known they'd come back."

"Child killer, but they're not talking about the kidnapper, are they?" The sick truth knotted in the pit of her stomach. "They mean me. They don't even know me. How could they be so cruel?"

"Takes all kinds. Some are gullible enough to believe everything they read in the paper or on the internet."

They wouldn't be the only ones to come to that conclusion. "Why do you believe me, Adam? No one else seems to."

"I know you?"

"That's not much of an answer."

"But it is the truth. No one could fake the fear and torment you're going through now. Besides, you talked of having kids the first time we made love. You said you wanted a large family and couldn't wait to get married and have a baby."

Only then she'd pictured Adam in that family.

Never had she pictured a situation like this.

HADLEY SENSED THE tension the second she stepped into the hospital room. Her mother looked upset and more sickly than she had yesterday. She was pale though her cheeks and eyes held a feverish cast.

Matilda was standing near the bed. Her eyes were red and moist with tears.

"Her brother Quinton is alive," Janice announced.

"Matilda lied when she said he was dead. Detective Lane is the one who finally set that record straight."

Hadley shuddered as old images rushed her mind. The pervert who'd tried to molest her fifteen years ago was now a seasoned criminal and Lila and Lacy could be at his mercy.

They had to find him. Matilda had to help them. Hadley had to handle this in a way that assured she would.

"It's good to have the truth out in the open," Hadley said. "I'm sure Matilda feels the same."

Matilda nodded and mumbled a greeting.

"Is there any news?" Janice asked.

"Nothing since we talked last night." Hadley walked over to her mother's bed and took her hand. "How are you feeling this morning?"

"My granddaughters are missing and I'm stuck in this noisy quagmire of a hospital. I feel exactly the way you'd expect me to feel."

"I meant physically, from the surgery."

"I'm fine. Get me out of here. I can't do anything to help you from this bed."

"You're getting well. That helps." Hadley lifted her hand to her mother's forehead. "You may have a little fever."

"I have a minor infection. It's nothing to worry about. The doctor will explain it to you. The nurse is supposed to call him when you get here."

"Where is the nurse?"

"Having breakfast in the hospital cafeteria. Matilda and I needed a little privacy."

"I told her the total truth," Matilda blurted. "I've apologized. I'll pay the money back she gave me for Quinton's funeral. I did wrong and I'll pay back every penny."

"It's not the money that matters right now," Hadley said. "It's not even that you lied about Quinton being dead."

"I explained that to your mother," Matilda said, her voice breaking as if she was on the verge of tears again. "He threatened to kidnap Alana and take her out of the country, said he'd sell her as a sex slave if I didn't give him five thousand dollars to bail him out of trouble."

A threatened kidnapping had worked for Quinton before. Had that emboldened him to do more than threaten this time?

"Listen carefully, Matilda." She waited until Matilda made eye contact. "We can't change the past, but it is imperative that you tell the truth now. Do you know where we can find Quinton?"

"I don't. I swear I don't. I would tell if I did."

"When was the last time you talked to him?" Adam asked.

"Monday afternoon."

"Where was he?"

"In my kitchen, but I swear this was the first time I've seen him since I claimed he was dead and paid him off. I wouldn't have let him come to the house then except he called and promised me he'd turned his life around. He sounded sincere."

"How did the visit go?" Adam asked, his voice steady and his tone more civil than Hadley could have managed.

"Okay. He was only there about a half hour. I didn't want Sam or Alana to come home and find him there."

"Do they think he's dead?"

"Yes. I told them he'd died in car wreck in Vegas and that his girlfriend hadn't let me know until after the funeral. They didn't like her, so they believed me.

I wanted him out of their lives for good, out of all our lives. Sam was young and impressionable. I couldn't chance Quinton leading him astray."

"Quinton is in Dallas," Hadley said, thinking out loud. "I need to inform Detective Lane of that."

"You won't have to wait long to do that," Janice said. "I've already called him. He's on his way to the hospital right now to question Matilda."

"I didn't do anything wrong," Matilda insisted. "I'd never do anything to hurt any child, especially not Lila or Lacy."

"I believe you," Hadley said truthfully.

"But the police won't," Matilda said. "They'll arrest me and take me to jail. It will be in the newspaper and Alana will be embarrassed. She'll feel ashamed to have her mother mentioned as a suspect. So will Sam."

"Cooperate with the detective, Matilda. If you do, they won't arrest you." Hadley actually felt sorry for her, but if Quinton had Lila and Lacy, Matilda could well be the key to getting them back.

The nurse returned and looked distressed to find them all in the room. "Is there news about the girls?"

"No, but we cleared up a few things about who might have kidnapped them," Janice said.

"That's good news," the nurse said as she checked Janice's temperature, pulse and blood pressure.

Janice dropped her head back to the pillow.

"Has Dr. Gates been by this morning?" Hadley asked.

"Very early this morning, before his first surgery. He asked that I let him know when you got here. Shall I let him know now?"

"Please do." Hopefully there wasn't a problem, but

he'd said Janice needed to stay calm and that wasn't happening.

The nurse made the call. "He wants you to meet him in the third-floor surgery waiting room in thirty minutes."

"Perfect. In the meantime, I'll buy Matilda a cup of coffee while she waits for Detective Lane." And to make sure she didn't cut and run.

"And I need to make a few phone calls," Adam said.

"Not so fast, Adam Dalton," Janice ordered. "I'd like to have a word alone with you."

JANICE SENT THE NURSE out of the room before she started in on Adam.

"Do you have no decency?"

Her tone was sharp. She was gearing up to take all this out on him. He could take it, but getting riled up wasn't what the doctor had ordered for her.

"I'm not a saint," he said, striving to keep this low-key. "But, yeah, most folks think I'm an all-right kind of guy."

"I disagree. You're taking advantage of a horrifying situation to insinuate yourself back into Hadley's life."

"I offered my help. Hadley accepted it. That's all that's going on here."

No way was he going into his and Hadley's past relationship with her mother. He couldn't have explained it if he wanted to.

"I knew when I met you that you were trouble."

Maybe he was more like R.J. than he thought. Not that Janice was an authority on Adam. The only time they'd been together was the night of the traditional meet-the-parent dinner.

It had been a week into their whirlwind courtship, only two nights after he'd asked Hadley to marry him.

Janice had made it plain then that she didn't think a marine about to ship out to Afghanistan was any bargain as a son-in-law.

"I don't want Hadley hurt by the likes of you again, Adam. You broke her heart. And now you just show up when she's frantic and vulnerable and pretend to be some kind of hero."

If that was true, it had been the fastest recovery of a broken heart on record.

"I'm not pretending anything, Janice. I only want to help if I can. You're in the hospital. The girls' father isn't around. I'd think you'd be glad Hadley has someone to lean on."

Janice's eyes narrowed. "What did Hadley tell you about Lacy and Lila's father?"

"Nothing. Is there something I should know about him, like why he's not as desperate as Hadley is to find their daughters?"

Adam didn't understand why the big secret. He was certain Detective Lane had asked about the girls' father and he wouldn't have settled for the brush-off Adam had gotten.

"The twins' father is none of your business. When this is over and the girls are safely home again, walk away from Hadley, Adam. Do it even if she feels indebted and asks you to stay. She deserves better than you."

He couldn't argue that. But he deserved a straight answer about why Lacy and Lila's father wasn't even concerned enough to be here. He'd ask again before they met with Fred Casey.

This time he'd demand the truth.

SHELTON LANE FIGURED IT was his lucky day when he saw both Matilda Bastion and Hadley standing in the hall outside Mrs. O'Sullivan's hospital room. This case seemed less like an abduction and more like a sick murder case with every new piece of information he uncovered.

Not that he was ready to make book on that fact yet, but Hadley O'Sullivan had definitely not leveled with him. He couldn't think of one good reason why a mother who was desperate to find her daughters would lie to the police when asked what should have been a simple question.

If his theory was right, Hadley O'Sullivan might just be the coolest liar and the best actress on the planet. And Adam Dalton was either in it with her or he was as gullible where she was concerned as everyone else around her seemed to be.

He could see how Adam could be taken in by her. Hadley was a damn good-looking woman. She had all the tools for getting under any red-blooded man's skin. A gorgeous mass of red hair that looked even more enticing when it was disheveled. Great legs. Bodacious breasts.

And she was smart enough that even if she was guilty, she might get off scot-free if he didn't play his cards right and follow every police procedure in the manual.

He walked up and joined them. "Hello, ladies."

"Any progress?" Hadley asked.

"None to speak of, but I'm hopeful that will change any minute now."

He studied Hadley. Her eyes were shadowed with the same torment he heard in her voice. That and the edgy fear that defined her had been constant since he'd first met her.

It was also what kept him hoping his theory was wrong.

"I need to see Hadley alone for a few minutes before we talk, Matilda. Why don't you wait here? Hadley and I will be in a small conference room just down the hall. I've already gotten clearance for us to borrow it."

Hadley and Matilda both agreed to the suggestion. Once inside the small cubbyhole of a room used by doctors to meet with patients' families, he closed the door behind him.

"Does this have to do with Quinton Larson?" she asked. "Matilda just admitted to Mother and me that he's in the Dallas area."

"Did Matilda tell you that?"

"She admitted that he was at her house late afternoon on Monday."

"Interesting."

"There's more," Hadley said.

He listened and made notes while Hadley filled him in on the details Janice had not shared in her brief phone call. He had to admit that the new developments made Quinton seem a considerably more credible suspect.

Still, he had questions to ask.

He put down his pen, put his elbows on the table and leaned toward Hadley. "Why didn't you mention earlier that you and Adam Dalton had once been engaged?"

"That was a long time ago. I didn't think it mattered."

"Did you break up with him because of another man?"

"No. We broke up because of another woman. I didn't do the breaking off. Adam did."

"Yet you got married and pregnant soon after the breakup and he's still single."

"How do you know when we broke up?"

"Your engagement was announced in the newspaper."

"My mother's doing, not mine."

"Are you saying you weren't engaged at the time?"

"We were engaged—briefly." She threw up her hands. "I don't see why any of this is important."

"Everything is important when children are missing. How long have you and Adam been back together?"

"We're not back together. I hadn't seen or talked to him since we broke up."

"And the man you hadn't heard from in over three years heard about the kidnapping and raced to the rescue."

"You were there when he showed up at my door."

"Right. You fell right into his arms. And he hasn't left your side since, not even to go home last night."

"He stayed with me last night because I was such a wreck I didn't want to be left alone in that empty house."

"Like I said, Adam's a very thoughtful guy. I can see why you'd want him back."

"I don't want him back. He knows that. He slept on the sofa with his clothes on last night. What little sleep I got was in the bedroom that my girls were taken from. This isn't a soap opera. My daughters are in the hands of a madman."

"Did Adam break up with you because you were pregnant with someone else's babies?"

Hadley jumped up so fast that her metal folding chair skidded behind her, banging against the wall as it fell.

"I get it, Detective. I get you. You have a sordid little mind and you think Adam and I got rid of Lacy and Lila so we could have a love fest without him being threatened by someone else's children having come from my womb."

"You're putting words in my mouth."

"To match the thoughts already in your head. Stop playing games, Detective. Find my girls."

She stamped out and slammed the door behind her.

She had a temper. That proved neither guilt nor innocence. It did demonstrate she was capable of losing control.

HADLEY WAS STILL FUMING when she reached the waiting room where she was to meet Dr. Gates. The complications were becoming more and more entangled, the emphasis of the investigation losing focus. Having Adam around was partly to blame for that.

There was a time she'd have given half her life to have him back. Now she could be losing the most precious parts of her life because he was here.

This time she couldn't blame Adam. His motives were pure. More than she could say for herself where he was concerned. The least she could do now was be honest with him about everything—whatever the cost.

Hadley located a seat in the crowded area and waited. After five minutes, she got up and paced. After fifteen minutes of doing nothing, her mind began to play tricks on her. She began to imagine everyone near her was the kidnapper.

A woman walked past her leading a little girl who looked to be a year or so older than the twins. The girl's hair was tawny-colored and straighter than either Lacy's or Lila's, but seeing her created a longing in Hadley's heart that was so intense it brought tears to her eyes.

If the kidnapper would only call and let her hear their voices.

Instinctively, she started to check her phone and make certain she hadn't missed a call. Her handbag. She didn't have it. She tried to think where she'd left it.

She'd hung it on the back of the chair when she'd sat down to talk to the detective. She'd gotten so caught up in her angry tirade, she'd forgotten it.

She spun around and retraced her steps, racing to the elevator. By the time she reached the tiny room, she was breathing hard and fast from the panicky run. She opened the door without bothering to knock.

Her purse was there. But not as she'd left it. A bulky brown package was stuffed inside the side pocket.

Her first name was printed in lopsided letters.

The same kind of letters that the kidnapper had used to write yesterday's note. This had to be from him.

The kidnapper was here in the hospital, perhaps only steps away.

Chapter Seven

Adam was standing in the east end of the fourth-floor corridor near the drink machine when he looked up and saw Hadley almost run into another woman at the other end of the hallway. He dropped the remainder of his soda in the trash can and ran to catch up with her. By the time she ducked into a room near the end of the long hallway, he was only a few steps behind.

He found her alone in the room, clutching a bulky package and so pale he thought she was about to pass out. Panic hit him, fear that she'd gotten bad news from the doctor. Or worse, it had been bad news from the police.

"What's wrong?"

"This." She handed him the package.

"Where did you get this?"

"Personal delivery—from the kidnapper."

"You saw the kidnapper?"

"I didn't see him. That's the problem. But he was here, in this very room."

"What makes you think that?"

"After I talked to the detective, I stormed out without my purse. When I realized that and came back, this envelope was in the side pocket."

Adam muttered a few curses under his breath. The

abductor was gutsy as hell if he'd walked right into the hospital to contact Hadley. He couldn't have known she'd leave her purse behind. Had he planned to just walk up and hand it to her?

That made no sense.

Hadley worried a silver ring on her ring hand. "If he was here, who's with my girls? They could be locked in a room somewhere by themselves? They'll be afraid. They'll cry for me and I won't come."

"Just as likely he left them with an accomplice," Adam said, throwing her a lifeline. Or was it the accomplice who'd delivered the message?

Matilda was the first person who came to mind. She'd been in the hospital. She'd likely been in this very room with Lane after he'd talked to Hadley.

She couldn't have counted on Hadley leaving her purse, but she could have taken advantage of it. More likely she'd planned to leave it in Janice's hospital room but then hadn't gotten the chance when they'd arrived.

The meeting she'd had on Monday with her brother could have been a strategy session or maybe just the opportunity he needed to enlist her. Or maybe Quinton wasn't involved at all. No one saw her with him on Monday. She could have carried out the abduction all by herself. The girls would have gone with her without crying, especially if she'd convinced them they were playing a trick on their mother.

Lane was savvy and experienced. He'd come to the same conclusions. Matilda was already on his radar.

Adam examined the envelope more carefully. "This feels like a phone and maybe a video case. Do you want to call Lane?"

"No. Not until I know what's in it. He made it clear

today that he considers me a suspect. He might decide I shouldn't be privy to the contents."

He ripped the tab and reached inside. As suspected, he pulled out a DVD in an unmarked plastic cover and a disposable phone that could've been picked up at any truck stop or convenience store.

"My laptop's in my truck. We can go down and play the video there. But once you've seen it, I think you should call Lane. There's a chance that the kidnapper was caught on a hospital security camera and Lane has the authority to confiscate the film."

"I didn't even think of that," she admitted. "I'll call the detective as soon as we've watched the video. Is that all that's in the envelope? No note to explain the phone?"

Adam checked again. "No note. Whatever he wants you to know must be on the disk."

He put a hand to the small of her back. His instinct was to put his arms around her, but the rules that defined their new relationship were vague and tenuous. He didn't want to do anything that she would misread and cause her to be uneasy with him.

She needed someone to trust. He needed to be that man. Semper Fi.

"I need to make a quick stop by Mother's room and let her know that I'll be staying at your father's ranch."

"She won't like it. She doesn't like much of anything about me."

"I know, but I need to keep her in the loop. I don't want her to hear from Lane that I've disappeared. I guess I should tell him where I'm staying, as well, although he has no trouble getting in touch with me by phone. Plus all my calls are monitored—which obviously the kidnapper realizes."

"Hold off on telling Lane where you're staying until

Fred Casey arrives. I'm not sure how he handles working with the police."

"I'd rather not say anything to Mother about the video yet. I'll call her after we see it—if it's good news."

The last of the words were only a whisper. More like a prayer, Adam thought. A prayer that echoed in his mind.

Dr. Gates approached them just outside her mother's door. "I was hoping I'd catch you before you left the hospital," he said. "I'm sorry I kept you waiting downstairs. The surgery took longer than expected."

"I understand. And then something came up and I had to rush off. Mother mentioned an infection. Is it serious?"

"Not if she stays on the infusion of antibiotics we're shooting into her bloodstream. But she keeps insisting that you need her and that she's leaving the hospital whether I release her or not. She's a very headstrong woman and you and her granddaughters mean the world to her."

"I know. I do need her, but I need her well and healthy again. I'll talk to her."

"I appreciate that. How are you holding up?"

"One minute I think I'm doing well, the next I think I'm losing my mind."

"I can prescribe something to help with the anxiety if you'd like."

"Maybe later, but not yet."

"My wife said to tell you that the members of her Bible Study group are all praying for you."

"Thank her for me. That means a lot."

The doctor left and Adam waited outside while she talked to her mother. He knew the visit would be brief this time. The video with the kidnapper's next message was calling.

There were dozens of hideous possibilities for what the video might reveal, scenarios that would destroy Hadley.

But there was a better chance they'd get directions for how the ransom was to be handled. He was counting on a nice, direct description of how he—or she—wanted the ransom handled. After that, Fred Casey would be put to the test.

HADLEY BARELY DARED to breathe as they took the elevator to the second floor of the hospital parking garage. Dread and anticipation battled inside her.

She so desperately needed this to be a plan of action for getting her girls back. Yet she could never escape the fact that as long as Lacy and Lila were in the kidnapper's hands, a million things could go wrong.

"Wait here," Adam said when they reached his truck. "I'll set the computer on the hood. That way we can both get a good viewing angle."

Once the computer was in place and up and running, Adam took the DVD from its case. "Are you ready?"

She took a deep breath hoping that would slow the rapid drumming of her heart. "I'm ready."

A haunting lullaby played in the background as the screen went from black to a shot of water drops falling on the camera lens.

The music stopped, replaced by laughing and the squeal of high-pitched voices. Lacy's and Lila's voices. Hadley's fingernails dug into the palms of her hands.

Then suddenly the close-up of water drops changed to a grassy square of land and a squirting water hose. Lacy and Lila were dancing in the spray. They were dressed only in training panties that Hadley didn't recognize.

But they were safe and laughing.

Tears of relief burned the back of Hadley's eyelids and then escaped to roll down her cheeks. The screen went black. The message followed.

"Your daughters are adorable, Hadley. It would be a shame for them to have to die. But that's up to you."

The chilling words were delivered in a disguised voice. A male voice, she thought, though she couldn't be sure.

Adam slipped an arm around her waist as the message continued.

"I will call you on the phone when I'm ready to exchange them for the five million dollars. Have the money ready. Any sign of cops or deceit and you will never see Lila and Lacy again. They send their love."

Adam called the messenger a few choice names. She agreed with them, but nothing could steal the respite that seeing the girls alive and happy had given her.

"They're alive, Adam. I can deal with anything knowing that."

The tears flowed like a summer rain, soft and warm on her cheeks. Adam's arms tightened around her. Her head fell to his shoulders and she gave into the need to be wrapped in his embrace.

Her girls were alive. She and Adam would get them back. They were in this together now and they'd let nothing stand in their way.

ADAM HATED THE EMOTIONS that erupted inside him. Feeling anything except empathy for Hadley was dangerous and would lead to complications neither of them were ready for.

Even if she wanted him back in her life, the reasons he'd walked out on her hadn't changed. If anything the chance of any kind of meaningful relationship had grown slimmer. Now they had the added strain of more than three years of distrust and resentment.

But it was useless to lie to himself. In spite of what he'd told himself time and time again, he'd never gotten over her. He doubted that any man could.

And yet her ex hadn't come running to her rescue the way Adam had.

The tears subsided and Hadley pulled away. His arms felt empty. The rest of him felt like he'd been kicked in the gut. With all they had to deal with, he was crazy to let her nearness get to him.

"I'd like to look at the video again," he said. "I'd like to study the more subtle details, see if there's any background or sounds that might suggest a location."

"I thought it looked like the kind of patio-size yard you have with a condo," Hadley said.

"I agree. It's too hot to stand around in the garage. There's a roadside park on the way to the ranch. We could grab a sandwich somewhere and sit in the shade to eat and study the video."

"I might even be able to choke down some food now that I know the girls are alive."

They seemed to be unharmed—for now. Though he wouldn't dream of saying it out loud, the kidnapper's message had unnerved him. No matter how good Fred Casey was, a thousand things could still go wrong with the transfer, especially since they didn't have five million dollars.

Fred had said they wouldn't need it. But Adam figured the kidnapper meant exactly what he'd threatened.

It was expertise and sanity against a madman. He didn't like the odds.

Adam powered down the computer. "Do you want to call Lane now?"

"Not now. You heard what the kidnapper said. No cops. I can't take chances. Besides, isn't Fred supposed to run the show from here on out?"

Adam checked his watch. "Yes, and his airplane should be on the ground at DFW by the time we get to the ranch."

The ranch and the reunion with R.J. As they say in combat, the easy way is always mined.

R.J. LADLED THE warmed-over chicken and dumplings into a cracked pottery bowl. The fragrant odors made his mouth water. He wasn't much of a cook himself, but his neighbor, Carolina, was as good a cook as she was pretty.

Every old man fighting a losing battle with a brain tumor needed a neighbor like her. Come to think of it, he wondered if his daughter, Jade, could cook.

Probably not. Her mother couldn't scramble an egg without it tasting like cardboard and that was a fact. She'd had other talents, though. He smiled just thinking about those.

All in all, he couldn't complain about any of the mothers of his six kids. They could sure complain about him, though. He reckoned most of them did.

One complaint they couldn't make if they were honest. He might have been late on some of his child support payments, but he never missed one entirely. Not even in the beginning when his bad habits chewed up his income like that old goat he'd kept around for a while back in the eighties.

Seemed like yesterday. That was the thing about time. It flies whether you're having fun or not.

R.J. set his bowl on the table and then went back for a spoon. His memory was less dependable by the day. According to the doctor, it would get worse. Not much to look forward to.

For a few weeks there, he'd looked forward to his five sons and Jade moving back to the ranch. Stupid of him to think he could force them into one big, close family when they had no use for him.

All but Adam had stuck around to ask a few questions yesterday. None had indicated they'd be back anytime soon.

R.J. picked up the remote and turned on the TV for the noontime news. He blew across a forkful of chicken to cool it as the commercial ended and the blonde newscaster smiled into the camera, making it look like she was smiling right at him.

Always nice to get smiled at by a good-looking gal even if the smile was fake and she didn't know he existed.

The lead story was about those two twin girls who had gone missing from the bedroom in their grandmother's house yesterday. A man who'd do something like that was just stirring up hell with a long spoon.

"...Adam Dalton, a veteran..."

"Whoa. What was that?" R.J. grabbed the remote and backed up for a repeat.

"No arrests have been made, but police say they're investigating several persons of interest in the case including Adam Dalton, a veteran of the war in Afghanistan who'd moved back to the Dallas/Fort Worth area less than a month ago.

"When our reporters tried to talk to Hadley O'Sullivan, she and Adam Dalton refused to comment."

"Well, don't that just beat all." Adam was mixed up with the mother of the missing girls. No wonder he lit out so fast yesterday. He wondered if Adam could be involved in the kidnapping.

Not likely. Jerri would have raised him better than that. Maybe he should give Jerri a call. He'd have to give that a bit more thought. Might be better to contact Adam and see if there was anything R.J. could do to help.

Maybe later, he decided. Only fools jumped into the fray when they hadn't been invited. Actually, he could be wrong about that. He supposed a good father might jump into trouble to help out his son on occasion.

He finished his chicken and dumplings and carried his dishes to the sink. If he was going to think this through properly, he'd have to go saddle up Dooley. He always thought better on the back of a horse.

Old memories invaded his mind. Adam had loved horses, too. From the time he was first walking, he'd been fascinated by them. R.J. would sit him in the saddle and Adam would grin like a possum. Never showed fear, that boy.

From what Meghan Lambert had learned about him during her investigation, Adam had never shown fear as a marine, either. That had almost cost him his life.

Hadley O'Sullivan was lucky to have him on her side.

HADLEY FORCED DOWN another bite of sandwich. She'd been hungry when she started, but no matter how much relief the beginning of the video offered, the ending always turned her stomach.

They'd watched it three times now, parts of it in

slow motion. If there were clues as to where it had been filmed, they were well-hidden.

"I've seen enough," she said. "I'm ready to go when you are." She wadded the rest of her sandwich into her napkin and carried it to the nearest trash can.

When she came back, Adam was perched on the top of the picnic table watching her. He patted the spot next to him. She slid onto the wooden table and rested her feet on the bench.

"I hate to bring this up again, Hadley, but I'd really like to have a better handle on your relationship with the girls' father before we talk to Fred. I know he's going to ask as I'm sure Lane did before I showed up yesterday."

"It was one of the first questions Lane asked."

"That makes sense, especially since it looks like an inside job."

"He's not involved. But I'm sure Lane followed up to ascertain that for himself."

"I'm not trying to be nosy. I just don't want any surprises at the last minute. Just tell me what you told the detective and I won't ask you again."

But she'd gone too far to settle for that. Adam had every right to know the whole truth. She realized that now. That didn't make this any easier. Now she had to figure out where to start.

"I was four months pregnant when Jim and I married."

"I didn't realize that. All I heard was that you were married and expecting."

"We separated a month before the girls were born."

"Odd timing."

"The marriage was a mistake. We knew it from the beginning. I was vulnerable and alone and there were health concerns connected to the pregnancy. Jim's a caretaker. He fancied himself in love with me and wanted be there for me."

"Sounds like a great guy."

"He is, but I wasn't in love with him. I didn't want to use him, so I decided it was time to stand on my own two feet—very swollen feet at the time. Besides, he had a job offer in California. I didn't want to stand in the way."

"Is he still in California?"

"Yes, and fortunately married to a wonderful woman. They have a new baby boy."

She slid off the table and moved a few steps away from him, hoping she could think clearer if he wasn't so near.

"There's more," she said. "I suggest you stay seated for this."

Chapter Eight

Hadley looked anxious and uneasy, as if she were afraid that the next step might send her flying over a cliff. Or like she was about to confess a cardinal sin. All of a sudden, Adam wasn't sure he wanted to hear more.

"You don't have to say more."

"Actually, I do. I should have found a way to get word to you years ago, Adam." Her voice broke and she turned away from him. "Lila and Lacy are your daughters. I was pregnant before you shipped out."

Adam heard the words, but it took all his powers of concentration to make them sink in. "Are you sure?"

"I'm positive. They couldn't be anyone else's. I hadn't had sex with anyone but you for over eighteen months before I conceived. I haven't been with another man since you."

"But the marriage…"

"Was a sham," making a statement of his question. "It was never consummated."

All the months he'd lain in that hospital, agonizing over her making love to another man, all the long nights when he'd survived on bitterness that she could forget him so easily.

Had she been clinging to the love they'd shared, resenting him, feeling betrayed as he had? But he could have never married someone else.

"Why didn't you tell me I was going to be a father? Why didn't you give me a chance to do right by you?"

"Don't turn this all around to me, Adam. I laughed and cried for joy when my pregnancy test came back positive. We were going to be married. We'd have each other and a head start on the big family I've always wanted. I couldn't wait to be a family."

"But you didn't even send me an email."

"No, I wanted to wait until I saw the doctor and was sure. The day he confirmed what I already knew, I got your letter. You'd met someone else."

Only he hadn't met another woman. He'd met an ambush. He'd become damaged goods. He couldn't move his legs and the doctors weren't sure he would ever walk again. Worse, he was still only half a man. He couldn't saddle Hadley with that. And he couldn't abide her staying with him out of pity.

Life was a bitch, especially for an injured warrior.

"I have two daughters," he said, his mind still struggling with that fact. And now they were missing.

"Suppose I hadn't shown up at your door yesterday," he questioned. "Would you have tried to find me and let me know that my daughters were in danger?"

"I don't know, Adam. I honestly don't know. I was shocked to see you. I didn't even know you were back in Dallas."

"I haven't been here long." But he'd been with her for over twenty-four hours. "Why didn't you tell me this yesterday?"

"I'm not sure."

"Is it because you don't trust me?"

"I think it's more that I didn't trust myself."

"And now?"

"I trust you to help find the girls, but that doesn't bridge the gulf between us. I don't really know you anymore. You don't know me. We both have new lives. We've moved on."

Only he hadn't, or at least his heart hadn't.

"Are you married?" Hadley asked.

"No. The military lifestyle doesn't foster long-term commitments."

"So it appears. But don't worry. I'm not planning on cramping your style. You can walk away when this is over. I can take care of the girls on my own."

Which would make him the same kind of father R.J. had been. Throw a little money in the pot to help support your children and then give them a call and invite them out for a beer when you know you won't live long enough to get to really know them.

He'd be damned if he let that happen.

"I'd like to be a part of their lives," he said.

He meant that, even if it involved staying in touch with Hadley. Even if it meant a constant ache to hold her in his arms and take her to his bed knowing that he could never satisfy her.

"We'll work something out," she said. "When this is over and the girls are safe at home with me."

Sadness crept into her voice where only fear and anxiety had been before. It cut him like a knife slicing into old wounds.

"Let's get out of here, Adam. I can't deal with this right now. And I've basically said it all."

His phone rang as they started back to the truck. "Hello, Fred. Welcome to Dallas. And not a minute too soon."

Adam caught Fred up to speed on the video and gave

him directions to the ranch. It'd be best for Adam and Hadley to beat him there so that Adam could let R.J. know he was about to get a lot more family trouble than he'd bargained for.

ADAM STOPPED AT the metal gate and the rusty metal sign that announced they were at the Dry Gulch Ranch. "This is it," he said.

"Where's the house?" Hadley asked.

"About a quarter of a mile down that dirt road you see in front of you."

"I'm not sure our coming here was the best option."

"I don't see any media blocking the road."

"Give them time," Hadley said.

Time was the one thing they didn't have much of— time and money. At least not five million dollars. He was eager to hear Fred's plan for how to handle the ransom exchange without the cold, hard cash.

Hadley opened her door. "I'll get the gate."

He drove over the cattle guard and she closed and latched the gate and jumped back into the truck.

"What's the ranch house like?"

He had a feeling she was making conversation, but that was okay with him and better than the awkward silence that had held most of the way to the ranch.

"It's your typical hundred-year-old raised cottage gone wild," he said. "It's been added on to so many times that it rambles like a patch of poison ivy that can't decide which direction to spread."

"In that case it should be large enough that we won't inconvenience your father. Does he live there alone?"

"As far as I know. There was no mention of a wife the other day—at least not a current wife."

"How many times has he been married?"

"I'm not sure. According to my mother he changes wives and family more often than she changes the sheets. Mother has been known to exaggerate."

Hadley stared out the side window. "I see lots of barbed-wire fencing, but I don't see any cattle."

"They're around somewhere." Adam pulled up in front of the old ranch house where he'd spent the first four years of his life. There was a black pickup truck parked in front of the house. If R.J. was there, he should have heard them drive up.

Adam climbed the stairs with Hadley at his side. He took a deep breath, exhaled slowly and rang the bell. No one answered. No one answered on the second ring or the third ring, either.

He tried the door. It wasn't locked. R.J. didn't seem the type to stand on formality, so Adam opened the door and walked in.

It felt a hell of a lot like he'd just entered the enemy camp.

MATILDA TOOK THE last pan of chocolate chip cookies from the oven and set the hot baking sheet on the cooling rack. She was in no mood for baking, but once she'd started preparing the dough, the familiar rhythm had a calming effect on her that let her think more clearly.

She knew exactly what she had to do. She'd preached the importance of truthfulness to Alana and Sam all their lives. Now she had to admit to them that she hadn't practiced what she'd preached.

The uncle they'd practically worshipped wasn't dead as she'd told them. He was alive and about to be arrested and possibly locked away for the rest of his life.

She'd explained everything to Detective Lane this morning. The faked death, the missing key, the recent visit from Quinton. And then she'd given him the names of the thugs Quinton had hung out with before he left Dallas. Once the web of lies had started to unravel, it was as if a staggering weight had lifted from her heart.

Her conscience was clear. But for the first time in her life, she was actually afraid of her brother.

Even though Quinton was six years younger than she was, he'd been the one to run interference for her when she was a young, skinny teenager.

Her little brother had thrown himself between her and her drunken father when he'd come at her with his belt for not having the house clean enough or not having his clothes washed or his dinner on the table. More than once, he'd ended up taking the beating that had been meant for her.

But by the time he was sixteen, Quinton didn't take a beating from anyone. And nobody crossed him without paying for it.

Matilda had crossed him today.

Alana strolled into the kitchen and pulled the earphones from her ears. "Sam said you wanted to talk to both of us. What's that about?"

"Go get your brother and I'll tell you over cookies and milk."

"Cookies and milk? We're not six, you know?"

"Too bad. You weren't nearly so sassy then. Go get Sam."

Alana tangled the ends of her long brown hair with her fingers. "It's about the kidnapping, isn't it?"

"Just go get your brother."

"First, tell me they're not dead. Tell me that creepy jerk that stole them didn't kill them."

"They haven't been found and there's no evidence

they've been killed. Now go and get you brother and I'll tell both what's going on with the investigation."

Alana returned a few minutes later with Sam. He grabbed a warm cookie and stuffed most of it in his mouth.

"Any luck with the job interview?" she asked, as she poured three glasses of milk.

"I didn't go."

"Why not? I thought you were supposed to talk to the manager right after your class."

"Because I'm not gonna spend my life stocking groceries." He finished that cookie and grabbed another.

"A part-time summer job is not exactly your whole life."

"It's not like I'm hanging around here all day doing nothing. I made forty dollars last week putting up new drapes for your boss. Man, those things were ugly. And summer school wastes half my day."

As if having to attend summer school wasn't his fault for skipping the class so many times that he had to repeat it before they awarded him his high school diploma.

Sam straddled a chair and grabbed another cookie. "So what's up?"

"It's about the kidnapping," Alana said.

Sam groaned. "Not that again. What's the big deal? Janice O'Sullivan is filthy rich. She'll pay the ransom for her granddaughters and never even miss the money."

"It's not about the money," Alana argued.

He grabbed another cookie. "It's always about the money."

"That's enough," Matilda said. "Will you both please just let me say what I need to say—without interruption?"

They both stared at her as if she'd spouted a giant

wart in the middle of her forehead. They weren't used to seeing her rattled and irritable. She counted to ten silently, determined to at least sound in control.

"There's been a development in the case that I think you should both be aware of," she said. "I hate having to tell you this, but…"

Adam slammed his half-empty glass to the table. "Don't tell me the cops think you had anything to do with it."

"No, but they do have a suspect."

Alana clapped her hands twice. "Thank goodness. I bet it's that Adam guy they talked about on the news. He didn't want to have to put up with another man's kids so he just got rid of them. My friend Karen thinks the same thing."

"Don't rush to judgment. The truth is…"

The doorbell rang.

Sam jumped up to get it.

"Let me," Matilda said. "Both of you stay put. It's probably Leone from next door. I'll get rid of her."

Lost in her thoughts, Matilda foolishly opened the door without looking through the peephole first.

"Hello, sis. Why is it you don't look glad to see me?"

Panic choked her. She gulped in a breath of air. "You shouldn't be here, Quinton."

"Why not? You've made no secret of the fact that I'm back in town." He sniffed. "Is that fresh-baked cookies I smell? If it is, I know a couple of little girls who'd love a taste of those."

Chapter Nine

"Uncle Quinton?"

"In the flesh."

Alana squealed and came running toward him, hurling herself into his arms. "I can't believe you're here."

"Seeing is believing."

"You're supposed to be dead."

"Just a bad rumor." He whirled Alana around a few times and then set her back down.

Sam joined them. Unlike Alana, he was speechless for a minute. And suspicious. "Man, this is weird." He turned to Matilda. "Mom?"

"It's your uncle Quinton, all right. I was about to tell you when he rang the doorbell."

"You knew," Alana asked.

"She just found out," Quinton said. "And I just got back to Dallas."

Sam still looked a bit skeptical. "Where have you been for the past five years?"

"Laying low. I'd gotten into a little trouble and had to leave town fast. Didn't want any of you getting dragged into it."

"But Mom said there was a funeral in Vegas," Sam said.

"It was a case of mistaken identity. But never fear, I'm back now. You'll see lots of me from here on out."

Matilda stood quietly, arms folded while Quinton made getting reacquainted with her children a celebratory occasion.

"How can you be so calm, Mom?" Alana asked. "It's like your brother came back from the dead."

Quinton threw an arm around Matilda's shoulder. "Your mother's a little upset with me because I haven't been in touch for so long. But she's plenty glad to see me, aren't you, sis?"

"Elated." Her attempt at enthusiasm fell flat.

"I love surprises," Alana said. "And having you home is the best surprise of all. There's warm chocolate chip cookies and milk waiting in the kitchen in your honor, Uncle Quinton. Just like a party."

"Bet he'd rather have a cold beer," Sam said.

"You know it." Quinton laughed and he and Sam exchanged a couple of playful jabs. "But I can't stay but a few minutes and I need to spend them talking to your mother in private."

"You just got here," Alana complained. "You can't just turn around and leave."

"We'll have plenty of time to talk later. I'm going to be around so much that you'll get sick and tired of me. Your mother and I are going to be teaming up in a little business venture."

"You have to promise," Alana said.

"It's a definite promise."

Matilda fought the dread as Alana went in for another hug and Quinton and Sam exchanged several playful arm punches.

Quinton waited until they could hear loud hip-hop coming from the back of the house before he reached over, grabbed Matilda's wrists and pulled her close. The move was intimidating. His hold was so tight that spirals of pain radiated up her arms and to her shoulders.

"You've been busy, sis, talking to cops, doing your best to pin that kidnapping on me."

"I didn't go to the police. Detective Lane came to me. I had no choice but to answer his questions. But I swear I didn't blame anything on you."

"Tell that garbage to someone stupid enough to believe it. I've got friends who don't lie to me, and they say cops are stalking them like rats after cheese, telling them they'll be in big trouble if they don't cooperate." He threw in a few vile expressions that he'd never used around her before.

"Let the girls go, Quinton," Matilda begged. "Tell me where they are and I'll go get them. You can clear out of town and disappear again the way you did before. I have some money saved for Alana's college. I'll give it to you. It's enough to get you out of the country and established somewhere south of the border."

He let go of her arm. "Now aren't you just the sweetest big sister ever. Of course, you can afford to be generous now. Only problem is I don't have those girls and you know it."

"But when you came to the door, you said…"

"Don't take me for a fool, Matilda. There's only one reason you'd sell me down the river. You're doing it to save your own skin."

"I don't know what you're talking about."

"Then let me give you the simple version. You kidnapped those girls. I know it. The police know it. Probably your good friend Janice O'Sullivan even suspects it. Who else could just walk in the house and walk off with those girls without setting off the alarm?

"Only you were never very brave so you haven't been able to pull off the ransom demand. When I showed up at your door, it was the perfect solution. You could sic the police on me while you figured out how to get the money and get away with it."

"You think I kidnapped the girls?"

"I know you did."

"That's preposterous."

"Is it? I'm surprised you didn't get tired of playing obedient servant to that rich O'Sullivan broad years ago. After all, why should Janice O'Sullivan have it all while you scrimp by?"

"Her husband earned that money, that's why. And I don't have to scrimp by when I'm not constantly bailing you out of trouble."

"I'm not here to judge you, Matilda. I'm just here to get my share of the deal. And to make sure you don't screw this up. Where are you holding them? I know they're still alive. You might kidnap them but you're too much a wimp to ever hurt them."

"I would never kidnap or hurt any child. You surely know that about me."

"I'm not asking. I'm telling you. I want my share. Two can play this dangerous little game of yours. Either I get cut in or you'll never see sweet little Alana again." His grip tightened. "And we're not talking some paltry ransom sum, either. You probably asked for a few thousand. But it's two million. You got that?"

"I didn't kidnap those girls."

"Like hell you didn't." He flew into a tirade of curse words. "Alana for half of the ransom. That's nonnegotiable. I'll be in touch. Soon."

He pushed her away and walked out the door without looking back. Once she heard his car back from the driveway, she stepped outside and leaned against the column that supported the overhang.

Her fingers shook as she pulled her cell phone from her pocket and called the number the detective had given her earlier that day. When he answered, she filled him in on the visit from Quinton.

"I'm glad you called immediately," the detective said.

"But if he comes back, what do I do? How do I protect myself and my children?"

"Call 911 and don't open your door. I'll have the patrol cop in that area put on alert."

That did little to relieve her fears.

"While I have you on the phone, I need you to clear up a detail or two about you conning Janice O'Sullivan out of five thousand dollars," Lane said.

"Okay."

"Have you ever asked Mrs. O'Sullivan for money under false pretenses before or after that occasion?"

"Absolutely not. I didn't even ask when she gave me money for Sam's braces or Alana's cheerleading competition in California. Janice offered. No, she insisted. She's always been very generous with me."

"But you admit that you asked her to pay for a funeral that never took place for a brother who wasn't dead?"

"I did," she admitted for the second time that day. "But I told you, I tried to pay her back. She wouldn't let me."

"And he never told you why he needed the money?"

"No. I told you this morning, he just said he owed it to someone who'd kill him if he didn't pay his debt. He was so bruised and battered when he showed up that I figured he had to be telling the truth."

"Whose idea was the funeral?"

"Mine. I wanted him out of my life. I didn't trust him not to hurt me or Alana or Sam."

"Any particular reason?"

The old fears interacted with the new and gripped her so hard she could barely speak. "Quinton said that if I didn't get him the money, he'd take Alana and sell her to a South American sex slavery ring. She was only eleven years old."

"Kidnapping. The same thing he threatened tonight," Lane said. "The only difference is that now she's sixteen."

"He didn't mention a slavery ring tonight," Matilda said. "But the implication was there. And he'd do it, too. I know he would. The brother I loved is gone. A demon took his place."

She'd never stopped praying for Quinton. She'd never stopped loving him—until now. Love and hate. She wondered how many families fought that crippling mix and all the guilt and denial it created every day of their lives.

"It seems kidnapping has always been on the table for Quinton," Lane said.

"Yes, but if he kidnapped Lacy and Lila, why is he threatening me if I don't cut him in? Why is he coming around here at all?"

"To throw us off. To frighten you so that you don't cooperate with the police. He could have any number of reasons."

No doubt. He was smart in all the wrong ways.

When the conversation ended, Matilda stepped back inside. She locked the front door and tiptoed back to her bedroom. She wasn't ready to field all the questions she was certain Alana and Sam would throw at her.

She pulled the locked metal safe from the top shelf

of her closet and set it on her bed. The dread grew all-consuming as she unlocked it and took out the black pistol that her husband had bought for her when they were first married.

For her protection, he'd insisted. He'd made her learn to load it and shoot it. He hadn't been able to make her like it. And instead of making her feel safe, it had frightened her. It hadn't been out from under lock and key since he'd died.

She trailed a finger along the short barrel and then gingerly let the tip of her fingernail scratch along the trigger. The thought of aiming the gun and pulling that trigger made her chest constrict until she felt her heart might be squeezed from her chest.

Could she pull that trigger and kill Quinton if her life depended on it? She wasn't sure.

Could she pull the trigger if Alana's life depended on it? Without a second's hesitation.

One by one, she slipped the bullets into the chamber. When she put the safe back into the closet, the gun was no longer inside it.

She took out her phone. There was one more call she needed to make tonight, this one to Hadley. She had to apologize for not telling her about the missing key the morning they discovered the girls were missing. She hadn't gotten the chance to do that this morning.

And she wanted to warn Hadley that Quinton was most likely the kidnapper. Her daughters were in the hands of a demon.

R.J. SPOTTED THE UNFAMILIAR pickup truck parked in front of his house a yard or two before he reached the horse barn. One of his neighbors might have gotten a new truck. Not that he was expecting company.

He bypassed the horse barn and let Dooley trot on up to the house. Definitely not a neighbor, he decided as he caught a glimpse of the sweet young thing with the fiery mass of red hair sitting on his porch swing.

She waved and he smiled. He waved back and then climbed off his horse and left him standing there. Wouldn't matter if he ran off. Dooley always found his way back to his stall before feeding time. Usually he just waited around on R.J., though.

"You lost?" he asked, as he climbed the steps.

The lady stood and walked toward him. "I'm Hadley O'Sullivan. I'm here with Adam."

"So Adam brought you out to the Dry Gulch. Don't that just paint a black dog blue?"

"Excuse me?"

"Pay my rattlin' no mind. I'm R.J. I guess Adam told you about me before he drove you out here?"

"He told me that you're his father, but that the two of you haven't seen much of each other over the years."

"Right on both counts. I'm sure sorry to hear your daughters have gone missing. I know you must be frantic."

"To put it mildly. But the kidnapper has made contact with us. They're alive and I'll do whatever it takes to get them back."

"My money's on you," he said.

The door opened and Adam and a rush of air-conditioned air came rushing out. For a minute or more, R.J. and Adam just sized each other up, neither saying anything.

He probably knew more about Adam than Adam did about him. His information had come from an unbiased source—private detective Meghan Lambert. Adam's had come from R.J.'s third wife.

R.J. spit a stream of snuff juice over the railing and extended his hand. "Good to see you, son. Does this mean you're taking me up on my offer to move to the ranch?"

"Not exactly."

"I didn't think so. That's okay. I know you and Hadley here got trouble up to your eyeballs. Details of the kidnapping were all over the news."

"Don't believe everything you read or hear from the media," Hadley said. "But the basic story is true."

"If you mean the insinuations that you might be involved in the girls' disappearance, I already disregarded that. You got that panicked-mom look stuck to you like chewing gum in a dog's hair."

R.J. turned back to Adam. "You're both welcome to stay as long as you like. I sleep in the first bedroom on your right as you start down the hall off the family area. There are two more on the first floor and three on the second floor. You and Hadley can have your pick."

"I appreciate that," Adam said. "Hadley couldn't step out the door at her mother's house without being swamped by reporters and cameramen."

"You can bring your mother out, too, if you like, Hadley," R.J. said. "No use to leave her imprisoned by those vultures."

"Mrs. O'Sullivan had surgery yesterday morning," Adam said. "She'll be in the hospital for at least another day. But there will be someone else joining us, a man named Fred Casey. He's going to help us negotiate a ransom exchange with the abductor."

"Local cop or an FBI agent?"

"Neither. He's a private ransom negotiator. Normally he works with big companies that operate in unsafe parts of the world."

"How did you a find man of that caliber so quickly?"

"He's the brother of a friend I served with in Afghanistan. He's on his way here from the airport now. I know I should have checked with you before barging in with an entourage, but time is of the essence."

"No problem," R.J. said. "Just make yourself at home. Literally. If you see anything you want to eat or drink, no need to ask. How about a cold beer now?" R.J. wiped his shirtsleeve across his sweaty brow. "I'm having one."

"Sounds like a good idea," Adam agreed.

"I'll take a Diet Coke if you have one," Hadley said.

"So happens I do."

R.J. left them alone to talk about him. He heard another vehicle pull up as he leaned over to get the soda from the bottom drawer. He grabbed another beer while he was at it.

He didn't know if he and Adam would find any common ground or not. But he sure hoped Adam didn't let Hadley down. She needed a hero in the worst way.

According to Meghan, Adam had saved lives before. No reason to think he couldn't do it again.

FRED HAD SET UP a headquarters of sorts in the upstairs sitting area. The room was large with windows that overlooked a corral and a fenced pasture where at least a half dozen full-size horses and several colts roamed.

He'd brought his own equipment with him—a computer, portable printer, folding wall board with an area map for flagging locations, and wires and mechanical parts and tools for tying the cell phone that the kidnapper had left Hadley in with his own phone.

Adam was impressed with his level of preparedness

and his professionalism. It was easy to see why the man was so successful.

While Fred had set up, Adam and Hadley had filled him in on all the facts, as they knew them. Then they'd all sat down to watch the video again, and again, and again.

After the third playing, Fred stopped it.

"Why do you think he's waiting so long to call me?" Hadley asked.

"He's an amateur at this. My guess is the abduction was a spur-of-the-moment decision and now he—or she—is trying to figure out how to get out of the country with that much money in their wallet."

"Can't he just drive across the border?" Hadley asked.

"It's not as easy to do that as it used to be. And he's probably figured after the fact that as soon as the cops know he has the money, every border patrol agent in the country will be on the lookout for a man carrying that much cash."

"What about a charter plane?" Adam asked.

"Same set of problems if he goes with an honest company. And if he goes with a dishonest one, the pilot may kill him for the money and dump him from the plane sans parachute."

"How do you know he's an amateur?" Hadley asked.

"He didn't hide the fact that he had a key. If he'd made it look as if he'd broken in, the field of suspects would have been practically endless."

"Is that all?"

"There's the fact that he didn't have an escape plan ahead of time. That way he'd have only have to risk one contact with you and there wouldn't be so much wait time for the police to spend tracking him down."

"Is there anything we can do to speed this up?" Hadley asked.

"As a matter of fact there is. He needs an escape plan. I'm going to give him one. A plan that will lure him into our trap instead of the other way around."

"I don't want to take any chances with the girls' lives," Hadley said.

"That's why we insist on my plan. I'll start work on that now. All I need you to do, Hadley, is to let me handle all conversation from here on out with the kidnapper. You can answer the phone when he calls, but after that, leave the talking to me."

"What about the ransom money? I don't have anywhere near five million dollars."

"How much do you have?"

"How much do you need?" They all turned to see R.J. standing at the door. "How much do you need to pull this off?" he asked again.

"Fifty thousand in twenty-dollar bills should be more than adequate."

"I'll go to the bank and get it now."

Adam was pleasantly shocked, but he didn't really want any charity from R.J. "I'll pay you back," he said. "I'll start making payments as soon as I get a job."

R.J.'s brows arched. "You don't have one?"

"I've only been out of the service a month."

Actually he'd had a couple of offers that he'd turned down. After the military, any job requiring him to be tied to a desk in a stuffy office seemed worse than landing in the enemy's stronghold.

"We'll also need a couple of small duffels," Fred added. "They don't have to be new."

"I can provide those, as well," R.J. said.

Fred grinned. "Then let's fire up the grill and start cooking. It's time to bring Lila and Lacy home."

Adam liked his optimism. And he loved the smile on Hadley's face.

But still they needed the kidnapper to call.

THE REMAINDER OF the afternoon dragged by. Adam felt the pangs of being left out of the loop. Even R.J. was contributing more to the girls' rescue than he was right now, and R.J. hadn't been told as yet that he was the girls' grandfather.

In spite of that, R.J. and Hadley had bonded surprisingly well. When R.J. had returned from the bank, fifty thousand dollars cash in hand, she'd accepted his offer to check out some of his prize horses.

After that, they'd cooked supper together. Baked chicken with purple hull peas and fresh tomatoes and corn bread that R.J. had baked in a cast-iron skillet.

Fred and Adam had cleaned their plates. R.J. and Hadley had barely picked at their food. No one had mentioned the fact that the kidnapper hadn't called.

Now that he thought about it, no one had even mentioned the abduction since they'd discussed Matilda's call confessing to the missing key and naming Quinton as the most likely one to have taken it.

The fears may not be spoken with every breath, but they were no less real. They were all very much aware that the worst enemy was the ticking clock.

Adam looked out the window and watched as twilight hovered like a black widow spider squatting over its prey. It was after eight—summer days in Texas held on as long as they could.

Hadley tossed the magazine she'd been rifling through to the sofa. "I'm going for a walk."

"Would you like company?" Adam asked.

"Sure, as long as you don't expect much in the way of conversation."

He joined her. They both walked in silence until they were almost out of sight of the house. Hadley walked at a racer's speed, arms swinging, her hair bouncing about her shoulders. Finally, she slowed her pace.

"I'd like to bring Lila and Lacy to the ranch once they're home again," she said. "I think they should get to know their grandfather before the tumor takes over and he starts to lose control of his functions."

"Did he tell you that's what would happen?"

"He did. He's handling it well, don't you think?"

"I haven't thought a lot about it."

"Do you think his other children will move back to the ranch?"

"I don't know enough about them to even venture a guess."

"What about you?"

He gave that some thought. "I never pictured myself as a cowboy."

"I have."

"When? You didn't even know my father owned a ranch until today."

"True, but you have that cowboy swagger. And you always wear jeans and boots. So you look the part."

"That's from growing up in Texas."

He recognized the conversation for what it was— an attempt not to talk about the danger and the anxiety that never let go.

He hadn't noticed it until she'd brought it up, but he did feel a lot more at home on the ranch than he'd expected. But if he did decide to stick around after the girls were safe, he and his father would have to deal with more kinks than you'd find in a nest of rattlesnakes.

He hoped to be a better father for his daughters than R.J. had ever been. He hoped he got that chance. But how could he stay in Dallas when being with Hadley and not touching her, or kissing her, or crawling into bed beside her would kill him?

"We should go back," Hadley whispered as if reading his mind.

Hadley turned and set a quick pace as they retraced their steps.

"Is that Detective Lane's car?" she asked when they approached the house.

"Looks like it could be," Adam said. "I can't really tell in the moonlight."

"Maybe he has news." Hadley broke into a jog, not slowing until she reached the driveway.

It was definitely the detective's car. Adam stayed a step behind her as Hadley raced up the steps and into the house.

They found the detective and R.J. in the kitchen. R.J. was sipping whiskey from a short glass. The detective was hugging a mug of coffee.

"Have you found Lila and Lacy?" Hadley's words were punctuated with short gasps for breath.

"No," the detective said, "but I've located Quinton Larson."

At last they were getting somewhere, though you'd never know it by the look of foreboding on the detective's face.

Chapter Ten

"Funny, I don't remember you calling for directions," Adam said once they were all seated around the scarred oak table.

"I've had a tail on you ever since you showed up on the scene, Adam."

"Glad to see you're doing your job."

"Just tell us about Quinton," Hadley said. "Does he have my daughters?"

"If he does, they're not with him."

Hadley winced as if the detective had hit her. Adam watched as the optimism that she'd exhibited after seeing the video disappeared in a cloud of dread that showed in every line of her face.

"They must be with him," Hadley insisted. "Where else would they be?"

"All I know is that they weren't in the house where Quinton has admittedly been staying and there were no signs that they'd been there."

Frustration burned in Hadley's eyes. "Even Matilda thinks he's the one who took Lacy and Lila."

"Does anyone else live in the house?" Adam asked.

"Two other guys. One is the owner. He claims Quinton's been hanging around there, but he's never seen Quinton with a kid. The other inhabitant was too stoned to be much help. But the neighbors we questioned verified that various men and women came and went in that house, but they'd never seen or heard any kids around the place."

"They could be lying," Hadley said.

"They could be," the detective agreed. "It's not the kind of neighborhood you'd want to walk in after dark. The neighbor on one side was just released from prison last week. But we searched the house thoroughly. There was no sign that Lacy and Lila had ever been inside the house."

"Does Quinton have an alibi for the night of the abduction?" Adam asked.

"He says he was in Fort Worth, spending the night with an old girlfriend. We're checking that out."

"Like she won't lie for him." Hadley clasped her hands together, nervously twisting her fingers. "Is Quinton in jail?"

"We hauled him in for questioning, but we don't have evidence to hold him unless we find something concrete against him. He swears he's innocent."

"Ever met a guilty man who didn't?" R.J. asked.

"A few," Lane said.

"A damn few, I bet." R.J. pushed back from the table.

"Quinton made a few accusations of his own," Lane said.

"What kind of accusations?" Hadley asked.

"He claims you paid him a visit in Houston six months ago."

"That's a lie. I would never go see him. Why would I?"

"He says you had a job you wanted him to do for you."

The detective had thrown out a line, fishing for information. Adam had a feeling that was what this visit was all about.

Adam propped his elbows on the table and leaned toward the detective. "Hadley's going through enough without you taunting her with hearsay. If you have something she needs to hear, say it straight and get it over with."

Lane's mouth twisted into a scowl. He didn't like anyone messing with his game.

"Hadley might want to hear what I have to say in private."

She shook her head. "Anything you have to say to me, you can say in front of Adam and his father."

"Then here it is in a nutshell. Quinton says you wanted him to get rid of your girls for you. Not kill them, mind you, just get rid of them."

"That's crazy," R.J. said. "What does get rid of them even mean? Toss them out with the garbage?"

"According to Quinton, Hadley asked about selling them on the black market. She said she'd heard of childless couples who couldn't adopt through regular channels who were willing to pay big bucks for twin girls. As cute, precocious and well-bred as Lacy and Lila were, she figured they'd bring a bundle."

Hadley's face reddened and the veins in her neck and forehead popped out like cords. Had she been able to reach Lane across the table, Adam figured she might have tried to choke him.

Adam was tempted to do it for her. He stood, towering over the sitting detective. "If your idea of good police work is to torment victims then you're doing a hell of a job."

"I thought Hadley would appreciate knowing what Quinton is saying about her."

"It's all lies," Hadley said. "Cruel, evil lies. The man is despicable."

"I'm not saying I believe him," Lane said.

"But you are repeating his lies," Adam said. "The next thing we know, we'll be reading them in the newspaper."

"I'm sorry that my visit upset you, Hadley. I wish I could have come with better news. But we're doing everything we can to find your daughters. You can rest assured of that."

"Then find them," she said, still so angry she was shaking. "Keep a tail on Quinton the way you did on Adam and me."

"Without question."

"I have one more question before you go." Adam stepped into the detective's personal space. "Where is Quinton staying?"

"I can't share that information. Play this smart, Adam. Don't go looking for Quinton. You get in the way and I'll have no choice but to have you arrested for interfering with the investigation."

If he got arrested, so be it. Fred would carry on.

R.J. hitched up his khaki trousers. "If you want to find the abductor, forget criminal records, false accusations and usual suspects. See who's got the most to gain and is arrogant enough to think he can outsmart all of you."

Not bad advice, Adam thought. R.J. might have a lot more on the ball than he'd given him credit for. His so-called father might be worth getting to know after all.

Adam would reserve judgment on that until things were back to normal around the Dry Gulch Ranch.

R.J. showed Lane to the door. Adam turned back to Hadley. "Lane is really starting to piss me off."

"At least the police are questioning Quinton."

"True, but I didn't like his attitude when he slammed you with you those ludicrous accusations."

"He could have been more sensitive, but I'm glad he told me about them. If Quinton is making up lies like that about me, he must be trying to transfer suspicion from himself."

"That's definitely possible."

"I think it's a lot more than possible. I'm convinced he's behind the abduction. I just wish there was something we could do besides wait for him to call all the shots. I hate that he's in charge of their fate."

"We're working to change that," Adam assured her. "When the kidnapper calls, Fred will be ready for him." It was Adam who wasn't doing his part. And Lacy and Lila were his daughters, too.

His daughters. Daughters he'd never seen. Never rocked to sleep as babies. He'd never taken them to the park and pushed them in a swing. Never read them a bedtime story. Never told them he loved them.

He'd never even seen them. What if he never did?

"The military called me a hero," he muttered. "They gave me medals to prove it. But what kind of man can't rescue his own daughters from an incompetent kidnapper?"

He felt Hadley's hand on his arm. He turned and she leaned into him, letting her head drop to his shoulder. A second later she was in his arms. He held on tight, knowing she wanted only his comfort.

The mother of his children. The woman who would always hold his heart in her hands. The woman he could never claim as his own as long as he was only half a man.

But, God, please let her have her daughters back. He'd gladly give his life for that.

SHE KICKED OUT of her shoes and stretched across the lumpy bed. "I saw Lacy and Lila's mother today. She's probably very pretty when her eyes aren't red and swollen. She wasn't wearing any makeup, either, not even lipstick."

"You got close enough to see all of that?"

"I was standing just a few feet from her."

"Did you have to get that close?"

"Don't worry. I was standing in an empty room just down the hall from her mother's hospital room. I only had the door open a crack. She couldn't see me."

"What the hell were you doing in the hospital? I never said for you to follow her around."

"I didn't follow her. I just waited outside her mother's hospital room until she showed up."

"I told you to locate Adam's truck or Hadley's car in the parking lot and then leave the package taped to the windshield. I even gave you the license plate numbers. Do you know how much trouble I went to to get those?"

"Do *you* know how many cars are parked in that lot? And they're constantly coming and going. I couldn't possibly check all of them."

"I gave you simple orders. Find the vehicle. Tape the package in place and then hang around to make sure no one took it before they got back to the car. What part of that did you not understand?"

"Don't talk to me like I'm stupid. I'm not stupid."

"You don't follow orders."

"No, but I got the job done. Hadley has the video. That's all that really matters."

He picked up his empty beer bottle and hurled it

across the room, missing her head by no more than a foot.

She jerked to a sitting position. "Don't you dare throw things at me! I'll walk out of here right now and tell the freakin' police where to find you."

"No, you won't."

"Try me. Or just keep throwing things against the wall and the people in the next room will call the cops and save me the trouble."

"In this dump? No one staying here wants the cops sniffing around."

"Yet you leave me and the girls alone in this scummy motel every night. You don't even care if someone breaks in and rapes me."

"Aw, baby, you know better than that."

He walked over to the bed and dropped to the edge of the mattress. When she turned her back to him, he reached around her and grabbed one of her breasts, thumbing her nipple until it puckered against the front of her low-cut T-shirt.

"As long as you eventually found the right windshield and the video and phone are in Hadley's hands, we'll be fine."

"It's in her hands." That part was true. "But I'm getting a really bad feeling about all of this."

"You worry too much, Mary Nell. You want the money as badly as I do. You were with me all the way when we decided to do it."

"That's when I thought it would all be over in two days the way you promised."

"It's only been two days."

"But we still have the girls and we don't have the money."

"I'm working on it. It's not as easy as I thought. I

have to make sure there's no way the cops will take us into custody or shoot us when we go in to get five million or when we cross the border."

"We're in over our heads. Please, let's just drop the girls somewhere in town. No one will ever connect us with the abduction."

"We can't give up now. We'll never have a chance to be this rich again."

"I know but I keep thinking what if someone did this to us? What if Lila and Lacy were our kids and someone stole them from us?"

"Stop bitching." He yelled a few curses.

Lacy woke up and padded over from her pallet in the back corner of the room.

"See what you did. You woke her up. And don't use that language in front of her."

"I want my mommy," Lacy said. "I want to go home."

"I know you do, sweetheart. And you are going home soon. I promise."

"You keep playing momma. I'm out of here." The door slammed shut behind him.

She went over, locked it and then pulled Lacy into her lap. "Do you want another story?"

"Yes. The princess story."

The princess who met her handsome prince, became unbelievably rich and lived happily ever after in a kingdom where they could entertain royally and dress in finery every day.

"Once upon a time…"

"How much feed per horse?" Adam asked as he made the rounds to each stall with the bucket of R.J.'s special feed mix.

"Two scoops, except for Hummer there on the end. He gets two and a third scoops."

"No wonder he's so big."

"The other way around," R.J. said. "He gets more feed because he is so big. I saw him in a show up in Nashville last summer and he was so magnificent I had to have him. I paid more than he's worth, but I like his style and his arrogance. Reminds of myself in my younger days."

"Does he give a good ride?"

"You know it. He's sensitive to every pull on the reins, but there are times he has a mind of his own. He likes nothing better than to gallop at full speed until he's panting for breath. Then he'll stop and look around as if to ask how I managed to stay in the saddle."

"I'd like to take him out one day and let him show me his stuff."

"I hope you will, Adam. When this is over, I hope you'll think about moving to the ranch. It would be a great place to ease back into civilian life. Lots of freedom. Not a lot of rules. Hard work, but I suppose you're used to that."

"There's no coddling in the marines." Adam gave one of the horses a good nose scratching as he tried to compare the man he was with to the one his mother referred to as trouble. So much trouble that she hadn't wanted him to have any part in Adam's life.

Evidently R.J. had mellowed significantly in his old age. That, or the brain tumor and knowing he didn't have much longer on earth had changed him.

Adam stopped to admire the big black horse. "What's his name?"

"Samson."

"It suits him. Have you always been interested in horses?"

"Interested? Yeah. But the passion's come since I got too old to pursue my first loves."

"Whiskey, women and gambling?"

R.J. tossed a pitchfork of fresh hay into one of the stalls. "My reputation always surpassed my exploits, but those were what kept me in trouble and causing trouble most of my life. Not that I'm proud of it, but I can't run from the truth."

"Then you don't gamble, drink and chase skirts anymore?"

"I drink a bit. You know that. You've seen me. I still go over to Shreveport on occasion and hit the casinos and I play poker with the other old farts around here once a month."

"And the ladies?"

R.J. chuckled. "I still notice 'em. I'm not dead yet. But the years take their toll on the old libido, Adam. I could chase, but I'd be like a puppy chasing a bobcat. If I caught one, I sure as shootin' couldn't handle it."

It wasn't only age that could affect the libido, but that was not a topic Adam cared to express with strangers. And his father was still a stranger, though he was sticking by Adam now the way you'd expect a father to do.

"It's none of my business," R.J. said. "You can tell me so if you've got a mind to, but what is the deal between you and Hadley?"

R.J. had just given him the perfect segue way to the truth. He considered coming clean, but at this point telling R.J. he was Lacy and Lila's grandfather would only complicate matters. It would be better dealt with when the girls were safe.

"We were engaged once. It didn't work out."

"Was that before or after you were injured in that enemy ambush?"

Adam froze and for a second he just stared at R.J. "How did you know about that?"

"Meghan Lambert is nothing if not thorough. She says you came close to dying, that it was a miracle that you lived and even more a miracle that you ever walked again."

He'd managed to keep the severity of his injuries even from his own mother. "What else did Meghan tell you?"

"That after you'd escaped the attack unharmed, you got shot when you went back into the fray and rescued two of your buddies from certain death. That you spent two years in rehab pushing yourself to the limits day after day, amazing all your doctors with your recovery.

"That you've spent the last year working at that same hospital where you did your rehab helping other wounded warriors push toward recovery."

"You're right. Meghan Lambert is extremely thorough."

"You broke up with Hadley when you realized you might not make it, didn't you?"

"Meghan didn't tell you that."

"No. I figured that one out for myself after seeing you two together. Too bad. Hadley seems like a terrific woman. I know she's hurting like crazy now."

"And it's getting harder for her every second that the kidnapper doesn't make contact," Adam said. "So let's just keep the info on my injuries between us."

"It's your life."

"And right now all I want to do is help Hadley get Lacy and Lila back. We passed the forty-eight-hour mark at some point during the night. I'm not sure how much longer she can hold up."

"Hopefully today will be the day when everything turns around. Fred Casey sure seems to have a handle on his end of the broomstick."

"One of the top in the country."

They finished feeding the horses and took the trek back to the house. A black, late-model Porsche approached as they reached the back steps. Adam didn't recognize the vehicle or the driver.

"Mighty early for company," Adam said.

"Those are the neighbors I was telling you about, Durk and Meghan Lambert. Actually they live in the city, but the family ranch, the Bent Pine, is only a couple of miles from here. I asked them to stop by."

"I suppose you have a good reason that doesn't include revealing my past to Hadley."

"Like I said, that's your business. Meghan would never step out of bounds. But Durk is the top dog at Lambert Oil and you know how good a detective Meghan is."

"They sound like great neighbors, but I'm not in the mood for making new friends. I can assure you that Hadley isn't, either."

"She might be when she hears what Durk and Meghan bring to the table. The Lamberts just brought a helicopter for ranch use and Lambert Oil has a couple of corporate jets. They might just come in handy if Fred still plans to lure the abductor into making a move that you control."

"Then let's invite them in."

Within five minutes the six of them were sitting around the kitchen table. Fred had been invited to the meeting. If the Lamberts did offer use of their helicopter and/or corporate jets, Fred would be the one deciding if and how they would use them.

Durk was definitely not what Adam had expected from a high-powered oil man. He was straightforward and down to earth. And Meghan proved to be exactly what Hadley needed, a female who wasn't connected with the investigation but was knowledgeable and sensitive.

"I know you're devastated, Hadley. I've followed the case as closely as I can, and it seems to grow more convoluted by the hour. That's why Durk and I called R.J. and offered to help in any way we could."

"I appreciate that, but I'm not sure what you can do that isn't already being done."

"I can investigate anyone you think could possibly be a suspect," Meghan said. "I don't follow the rules the cops do, and I have friends in high places—right up to the top of the FBI feeding chain."

"I don't know who I'd suggest you investigate. It seems to me that Detective Shelton Lane is covering all the bases."

"What about Alana and Sam Bastion? From what I've read, the police seem to be ignoring them."

"I can't believe either of them is involved in this. Not Alana for sure," Hadley said. "She's a sweetheart. She babysat the girls a few times."

"What about Sam?"

"From everything I know about him, he's a good kid. Mother hires him to help out at the house when she has a task requiring brawn. Nothing has ever come up missing when either of Matilda's children is around."

"Still, it might be good to see what I can find out about them," Meghan said. "If I find anything alarming I'll tell you and turn it over to Detective Lane," Meghan said.

"Yes, you will," Durk agreed. "I considered having that put in the marriage vows. Meghan will not put herself into danger."

"I did tend to do that in the past," she admitted. "But not anymore. I have more than myself to keep safe." She rubbed a baby bump by way of explanation.

"Then I accept your help," Hadley said.

"R.J. said something about a helicopter and corporate jets," Adam said.

"They're absolutely on the table if you need them," Durk said. "I can supply a pilot, fuel and whatever else you need to get those babies home safely. If you need cash to use as bait, I can help with that as well."

"Why?" Adam asked. "Why stick your neck out when you don't even know us?"

"It's the cowboy way," Durk said.

"But you're a businessman."

"My job is CEO of the family oil business. My love is the ranch. That makes me a cowboy."

"Fair enough."

"What are you planning to do now that you're out of the service and back in the States, Adam?"

"I'm not sure."

"If you're looking for a job, drop by the office one day. I'll hook you up with personnel and we can see what they can come up with that fits your interests and expertise. No pressure, of course."

"I guess giving out jobs is more of the cowboy way."

"No, I'd only hire you if you were a fit for the position and for the company. But we hire a lot of veterans. They have good work ethics and a strong sense of loyalty. And we all owe you a debt of thanks."

"In that case, I appreciate the offer, but the only thing I can concentrate on now is rescuing Lacy and Lila."

"I understand completely." Durk turned his attention to Fred and described the aircraft. "If you can use any of that, just let me know."

"I'm thinking that the helicopter or perhaps the small jet might be useful."

Durk pulled two business cards from his pocket. "This is my brother Tague's number. He's at the ranch all day today. He can fix you up with the helicopter. And this is my card. Call me if you need either of the corporate jets. I've already checked. They're both available and reserved for your use."

"How much notice will you need?"

"I'll give Tague a call now and tell him to get a pilot on standby for the helicopter. Or for that matter, Tague can fly it for you. So I'd say the helicopter could be ready by the time you drive to the ranch to board it. I'll need an hour's notice on the jet."

"Sounds good," Fred said.

They said their goodbyes and R.J. and Adam stood on the porch as Durk and Meghan drove away.

"Thanks for asking them to stop by," Adam said. "If you'd asked first, I would have probably said no. But I'd have never expected them to be so willing to do whatever it takes to find two kidnapped girls they don't even know."

"And the rest of the Lamberts are just as friendly and accommodating. Considering the life I've lived, it's amazing they have anything to do with me."

"Were you that bad?"

"I did a lot more hell-raising than I did volunteering my help. And as you know, I wasn't much of a father. That's why it's asking a lot to expect you or any of your half siblings to give me the time of day, much less move onto the ranch."

"You sweetened the pot with the money and the ranch."

"Money doesn't make up for letting people down. I can't undo any of what I've done, but I'd do a better job of being a dad if I had to do it over again. That's all I'm saying."

"That's saying a lot."

"Well, I lied. It's not all I'm saying. I've made lots of mistakes in my day, son. I've learned things the hard way, so trust my advice. Don't you let Hadley get away from you, boy. If you do, you'll be a bigger fool than I ever was."

Advice Adam would give the world if he could heed.

But he couldn't. Still, R.J.'s advice lingered in his mind as he walked outside and made a call to his mother. He wouldn't talk to her about R.J., but he did need to fill her in on what was going on.

He wondered if she suspected that he was still in love with Hadley when she'd called and insisted he offer his assistance. She'd always had a sixth sense about knowing what what was on his mind and in his heart.

R.J. might be new at being a Dad, but Jerri had been his mother all his life.

SMOKE FROM FRYING tortillas filled the Mexican restaurant. Quinton waved it away with his napkin and took a bite of the spicy egg, cheese and bean taco. This was his favorite breakfast dive, but today he was too agitated to even flirt with the owner's pretty young daughter who was back to refill his coffee cup.

Matilda had the means, motive and opportunity to kidnap those girls. She also had the motive to try and pin it on him—if she was guilty. But as hard as he'd tried to believe that she was the abductor, the edges of the puzzle always came out lopsided.

Matilda was loyal to the core. That's why she'd put up with so much from him over the years. She was also loyal to Janice O'Sullivan. It had almost killed her to con Janice out of five thousand dollars to bail him out of trouble.

The only reason Matilda had gone through with the scheme was to protect Alana from him. She would have never done it for herself.

So if she was willing and even eager to pin this on him, she must be protecting someone. But who?

"Hadley O'Sullivan?" He had no use for that bitch, but it was hard to imagine she'd gotten rid of her own kids. She'd definitely never called him and asked him to do it for her.

But the detective's eyes had lit up at that accusation. It was obvious he already suspected she had something to do with the kidnapping. It wouldn't take much to nudge him into arresting Hadley. But Matilda wouldn't pin the murder on him to protect Hadley.

So who took the girls? Adam Dalton?

Maybe. Tough former marine chasing hot mother of twins under the age of three. He might prefer to have Hadley all to himself. But the man had to know that if Hadley found out he'd gotten rid of her kids she'd never have anything to do with him.

So…

The owner's daughter came around again, this time with extra salsa. The girl was working her tip. Her mother probably didn't pay her near enough.

And all of a sudden the truth hit Quinton. He knew

exactly who'd kidnapped those girls. All he had to do was find the hideaway and he was in the game with four aces and a wild card up his sleeve.

Chapter Eleven

"I don't understand why you insist on staying on some hot, isolated ranch in the middle of nowhere that smells of manure. With Adam Dalton and his father no less."

"I've explained that, Mother."

"And it made sense when you were all alone, but I'm getting out of the hospital today. We can lean on each other as we've always done. We can see this through together."

"I'm not just here with Adam and his father. I told you that Adam has hired a professional negotiator to help us deal with the kidnapper."

"If Adam can afford this negotiator, then I'm sure I can."

"But you don't have access to a helicopter or corporate jets that might help in Lacy and Lila's rescue."

"And Adam and his father do?"

"The Lamberts of Lambert Oil are friends and neighbors of Adam's father. They've offered whatever we need."

"You've told Adam the truth, haven't you? After the way he treated you, you've come crawling back to him. That's why he and his father are taking over."

"I'm not crawling, Mother, but I would if it could get Lacy and Lila home safely. And, yes, Adam knows he's their father. I couldn't very well keep it from him when the girls are in danger. We haven't told his father as yet, but I'm considering it."

Janice started to cry. "I'm sorry, sweetheart. So sorry you had to make that choice. And I don't mean to fuss. It's just that I'm so upset. I just want them home again."

"I know, Mother. I know. It's going to happen. We're going to make it happen."

"Are you sure you don't need me to come out to the ranch?"

"I'm positive. You go home with your friend Karen and take care of yourself. I promise I'll keep you posted. When we get the girls back, you'll be the first person I'll call."

Janice sobbed into the phone. Hadley fought not to dissolve into tears with her and make this even harder on both of them.

"I know I shouldn't hate Adam, but he broke your heart and he never gave it a second thought. Now he'll never be out of your life."

And in spite of all he'd put her through, having Adam in her life would be perfectly fine with Hadley.

But before she could let herself dream of that, they had to find Lacy and Lila and save them from a madman.

Without warning, the terror took over. Hadley began to shake as terrifying images of her daughters locked in a room with Quinton infected her mind.

ADAM WALKED INTO the kitchen and found Hadley leaning against the counter, her body racked with sobs. His heart plunged to the depths of his soul as the worst possible scenario stormed his mind.

He tugged her around to face him and then took her in his arms. "Did you hear from Detective Lane?"

"No, just Mother. She cried and then I started thinking about Quinton and crying and now I can't stop." Her words were broken by the sobs, but relief washed over Adam. There was no news which meant as far as they knew the girls were still alive.

"I'm going crazy," Hadley said when she could finally talk without breaking down. "Whoever the kidnapper is, why won't he call? Why is he tormenting us like this?"

Adam picked up a napkin and began wiping her tears away. He hurt for her as well as for himself, but he knew meaningless platitudes wouldn't help. He stuck to the facts.

"We've heard from him every day the girls have been missing. Surely we'll hear from him soon."

"In the meantime, all I can do is wait and go out of my mind."

"You need to get out of this house. I was thinking about taking a quick horseback ride. How about joining me? R.J. has plenty of mounts to choose from."

"Thanks for the offer, but no. I don't want to leave the house in case the kidnapper does call. Besides, if I tagged along, I'd be such a downer it would defeat your purpose in going."

"Knowing you were here crying would ruin my ride far more. We don't have to talk at all if you don't want to, and we won't go far. You'll have your phone with you and we can get back to the house in minutes if there's a need."

"I haven't ridden in years," she said.

"But you have ridden before?"

"I rode a lot during my early teen years. The family

of my best friend owned a ranch in the Hill Country. They frequently took me with them for long weekends and summer vacations. I always hoped that one day I'd live on a ranch."

R.J. would probably love to give her Adam's share of the ranch. He just might when he found out that Lacy and Lila were his granddaughters.

"You could use some fresh air," Adam urged. He was going stir-crazy. She had to be feeling the same way. Doing nothing in the face of a tragedy was the hardest task of all.

He'd grab some food from the kitchen to take with them. At the very least he should be able to get her to eat enough to keep her from collapsing. He wasn't doing much else to help.

Being useless was killing him.

R.J. SADDLED A couple of horses that needed exercising while Adam made fried-ham-and-egg-on-toast sandwiches and Hadley changed into more comfortable riding clothes.

In minutes they were on the worn horse trail to the swimming hole. It was only mid-morning but the temperature and humidity were steadily climbing.

Adam led the way, taking his horse to a canter and then a full gallop when he realized Hadley had no trouble keeping up. They didn't slow until the old swimming hole came into view. Oddly the only part of it that looked familiar to Adam was the rope hanging from the branch of an oak tree that extended over the spring-fed pool.

They dismounted and Adam looped and secured their reins to the branch of sycamore tree.

"Your gnarly rope is still there," she said.

"Most likely it's not the same one. That was a lifetime ago." Last week was a lifetime ago.

Hadley walked toward the pool. Adam took the sandwiches and two bottles of water from his saddlebag before following her across the carpet of grass and weeds.

Hadley stopped to watch a butterfly flutter past. "The girls would go wild with this much room to run and play and a pool of cool water to wade in."

"The girls *will* love it here," he corrected. "R.J. is smitten with you. I'm sure he'd love for you and the girls to come out as often as you like."

"He's already said as much," Hadley said. "I feel guilty not telling him that the girls are his granddaughters. But if Lane finds out that you're Lacy and Lila's father, he'll find a way to twist that into suspicion and motive. Based on the fact that I lied about it earlier, if nothing else."

Adam had no doubt that Lane would find out soon. The longer this went on, the less likely he was to keep any of his secrets. He'd only glanced at the morning paper, but it was full of speculation about what had happened to the girls. He figured the TV and radio news was, as well.

Dallas citizens who believed that Hadley was innocent were worried about their own children and demanding the police move faster in solving the case and finding the girls.

The number who believed Hadley had gotten rid of her own daughters was growing and they were demanding an arrest.

And all Adam and Hadley could do was wait. He hated that the kidnapper held the reins. All Adam's military training, all his combat experience was worthless in this situation. He couldn't sneak up on the enemy or go rushing in with guns blaring. Even if they knew the identity of the kidnapper, a wrong move could get the girls killed.

So the best he could do was try to keep Hadley from falling apart. He unwrapped the top of a sandwich and tried to hand it to her.

She shook her head. "I can't eat."

"Try a few bites. You have to stay strong for the girls. You don't want to be fainting from hunger and exhaustion when the kidnapper calls."

She relented and reached for the sandwich. "I'll take a bite, but I can't guarantee that it will stay down. Even the sight of food makes me nauseous."

She took a bite, chewing as she walked to the water's edge. "Did I tell you that both Lacy and Lila can swim?"

"You never mentioned it."

"They can. I took them to toddler lessons at the YWCA last March. Lacy pretended she was a fish from one of her favorite movies. She wasn't the least bit afraid. In fact, she came up giggling when her head went under for the first time."

"Yep, she's my daughter. What about Lila?"

"She was a bit more cautious. She cried the first few times she got water in her eyes. But after the second lesson she was over her fears and reluctance. After that, she loved her lessons. And the hideous neon yellow swimsuit that she picked out herself."

For once talking about them wasn't making Hadley cry. In fact, it seemed to help. "What else should I know about my daughters?"

"Lacy loves to play outside. We walk to the park almost every evening in the summer. And she loves animals. She's been begging for a puppy but we'll have to move before she gets one. Condo restrictions forbid it where we're renting now."

"Every little girl should have a puppy," Adam said.

"The condo is all I can afford. I do the best I can by them on just my salary."

"That didn't come out the way I meant it," Adam said. "I'm sure that you're a wonderful mother." He'd never had any doubts that she would be.

"What does Lila like?"

"Her dolls and playing house and dress-up. She has this stringy-haired doll that she named Amanda. She never goes anywhere without it."

"The doll she was holding in the video?"

"That's the one. I'm so glad she has Amanda with her now. She would have cried herself to sleep every night without her. She might be crying now. She and Lacy could be locked up and alone with no one to hear or care if they're hungry, or hurt, or afraid."

Hadley's voice grew unsteady. Her body swayed. Her face grew ashen.

Adam caught her just before she sank to the grass. He lifted her and held her in his arms. She felt fragile, as if she might break if he held her too tightly.

"I've got you," he whispered. "I won't let you fall."

But that was the best he could promise. All they could do was take this one day, one hour, one second at a time.

"I think I should sit a minute before we ride back," she said.

"I agree." He led her to the base of a towering pine. Still holding his hand, she eased down to the carpet of pine straw. She straightened her back and held her head high as the color slowly returned to her face.

"I can handle this," she said. "I will not let the kidnapper win."

"That's my girl."

The girl who got away.

His phone vibrated. He pulled it from his pocket and checked the caller ID. Matilda Bastion. He retreated back to where the horses were waiting and took the call, keeping his voice low. If this was news about Quinton, he might need to break it to Hadley gently.

"Adam, it's Matilda." Her voice was strained. "I hope you don't mind me calling you, but I didn't know who else to call."

"I don't mind. I told you when I gave you my phone number to call anytime you feel the need. What's wrong?"

"Detective Lane was here again."

"To talk about Quinton?"

"No. He came to question Alana and Sam. He insisted on talking to each of them alone. I shouldn't have let him."

"Why is that?"

"He bullied them, treated them like common criminals. They were both nervous wrecks when he left. Alana was crying. Sam was so upset he put a fist through a wall. He just left for his summer school class. I'm afraid he might do something foolish like not come home tonight—or try to find Quinton."

"Did he mention Quinton?"

"He said he understood why Quinton hates cops. I was hoping you could talk to him and try to calm him down before he does something that makes him look guilty."

"I'd be glad to. Where's his school and how will I recognize him?"

She gave him the information and the time Sam's class would finish for the day.

"Alana's freaking out, too, but I can handle her," Matilda said. "She said the detective was trying to trick her into saying things she didn't mean to say."

"He's likely just doing his job."

"But why go after them instead of arresting Quinton?" Matilda protested. "There's no way they could be involved. They're both here all night, every night. I told him that. And they've never been in trouble with the police."

"Never?"

"*Almost* never. Alana shoplifted a lipstick from the drugstore when she was twelve. The clerk called the police and the officer scared her so bad she claims she's never even eaten a grape in the produce aisle since."

"What about Sam?"

"He's never been arrested."

"Still, maybe you should get a lawyer."

"I called one this morning," Matilda said. "My friend Johnny gave me the name of one of his customers who's a defense attorney. I'm waiting on him to call me back. But I thought I should ask you first. I was afraid lawyering up would make all of us look guiltier."

"I think you'd be wise to hire an attorney."

"Then I will. I never thought it would come to this, especially after I cooperated with the detective and basically told him how to find Quinton."

"Are you saying that you know where Quinton is staying?"

"I don't have an address, but I gave Detective Lane the names of the thugs Quinton hung out with when he lived in Dallas before. I even gave him the names of the sluts he'd dated—at least the ones I knew about. And I told him the names of some of the bars where Quinton used to hang out."

"How did you know those?"

"He used to talk about them. He liked playing the part of the good-time guy until he'd run into trouble and need help from me. I was the enabler. I knew that even then, but it's hard not to help your only brother when he's in trouble and begging for your help."

"Give me the same information about Quinton that you gave the detective, Matilda. Start by describing him in detail for me so that I'll recognize him if I run into him on the street. Height, weight, tattoos. Leave nothing out."

"He'll be easy to spot. His arms and even his neck are covered in tattoos and there's an old, jagged scar that runs from his hairline down his right cheek from where our drunk father took a knife to him when he was ten years old."

So Quinton had learned his ways from his father. That explained a lot. But then some of the guys Adam had served with in the military had similar stories from their youth and had turned out to be model marines.

In the end, it was all about the choices they'd made.

"You don't want to get involved with Quinton, Adam. He's guard-dog mean and he's got friends who are just as mean or meaner. Quinton used to brag that one of them shot and killed two unarmed men in cold blood and got away with it."

"I fought the Taliban for years, Matilda. I'm used to mean. Just give me the information."

"Okay, but don't say I didn't warn you."

"I consider myself warned."

Finally, there might be something he could do to help rescue his daughters.

SAM HAD BEEN so nervous after talking to Lane that he'd rammed his fist through the wall. That fact played and replayed in Adam's mind all the way into Dallas. That was why the school where Sam was taking summer classes was his first stop.

Adam watched as students left the building in clusters and took the walkway to the parking lot. Finally he spotted him, walking with two other young men about the same age and height as he was.

He was dressed as Matilda had said, but Sam was not the clean-cut, innocent-looking kid Matilda presented him as. He was at least a couple of inches over six feet tall, muscled, and he needed a shave and a decent haircut.

He parted from the other two guys in the parking lot and climbed behind the wheel of a Buick that had seen better days several years ago, the same car Matilda had said he'd be driving.

Adam pulled in behind him and followed him out of the lot. It was possible that Sam might lead him back to the Bastion home. But Adam had a strong hunch that Sam might lead him straight to his uncle Quinton.

Sam took the I-20 freeway and exited east of downtown. Adam kept on his tail but a few cars back until Sam pulled into a parking spot in front of a pawnshop in one of Dallas's seedier areas. Adam parked a few spaces down from him, staying behind the wheel of his truck until Sam entered a small, neighborhood café.

Adam took a cold beer from the cooler in the bed of his truck. It was important to fit in when hanging out on the streets of a neighborhood like this one.

He found a spot in the shadows of a decaying building across the street from the café. He could easily see who came and went and had a view of some of the

booths through the large, dirty windows that lined the
front of the café.

Sam took the last empty booth along the row of windows. Adam moved a few steps to the right so that he
had a better view. He pulled the bill of his Dallas Cow-
boys cap low over his forehead and slouched against
the building.

He watched as Sam spoke to a waitress. She returned
a few minutes later with what appeared to be a Coke
over ice. Sam pushed a straw into the drink and sipped,
but his gaze stayed focused on the front door as if he
were waiting for someone.

Hopefully, Quinton.

Sam finished that drink and ordered another without
ever looking at the menu.

Twenty minutes later, he still hadn't ordered and no
one had joined him. But there was no way Sam had
driven fifteen miles to order a Coke and drink it by
himself.

When the waitress brought Sam the tab, Adam decided he'd waited for Quinton to show up as long as he
dared. He crossed the street, walked into the café and
straight to the booth where Sam was leaving money to
cover his tab.

Sam paid no attention to him until Adam was standing directly over him, blocking his way out of the booth.

He looked up at Adam. "You got a problem, man?"

"No, I'm just here to talk."

Sam tried to push past him. Strength was on Sam's
side, but Adam had the advantage since Sam was
hemmed in between the booth and the bench.

Adam shoved him back into his seat. "You're a long
way from home, Sam. What brings you to the hood?"

"None of your business. You're not a cop."

"What makes you so sure?"

"I saw your picture in the paper. You're Hadley O'Sullivan's boyfriend."

"You just won round one."

"My mother told you to follow me, didn't she?"

"Oops. Lost round two. I'm here on my own. Now answer the question. What are you doing in this hell-hole neighborhood?"

"Spreading the wealth."

"Try again."

Sam spread his hands in front of him, palms up. "Okay, you got me. I'm here to buy some crack like most everyone else in this greasy dive. But don't run tattle to Mom. She doesn't really want to know, plus she's got enough worries right now. So do you."

"Here's the problem, Sam. I don't think you're here to buy crack or anything else. I think you're here to meet your uncle Quinton."

"What if I am? Is there a law against that?"

"There's a law against stealing little girls from their beds and trying to collect a ransom for them."

"You're not pinning that on me. Man, I'm clean. I'm not crazy enough to get involved in a kidnapping."

"Here's a shocker, Sam. I don't believe you. So let's make a deal, man-to-man. You tell me where to find Quinton or the missing girls and I won't call Detective Lane and tell him where you are right now. I won't even mention that I've got evidence to prove you're working with Quinton."

"You've got no proof of anything. I'm not working with my uncle. No way. I know what you're trying to do, but you're not getting me to confess to kidnapping."

"Too bad." Adam took out his phone. "I guess we'll just have to let Detective Lane work this out."

Sam put his hand on top of Adam's as he started to punch in the phone number. "I'll tell you how to find my uncle, but I swear I don't know anything about that kidnapping."

That remained to be seen.

QUINTON STOOD HIDDEN behind a Chevy van, watching as Adam and Sam stepped out of the café and into the glaring sunlight.

He had no doubt that Adam had followed Sam here hoping that he'd lead him to Quinton. Fortunately Quinton was too smart for him. He'd expected and prepared for something exactly like this. He'd spotted Adam even before he'd finished his beer.

Quinton would catch up with Sam. He'd make damn sure that Adam didn't, at least not in time to get in Quinton's way. The man might be tough when he had his marine buddies to back him up, but he was on Quinton's turf now.

All it would take was a phone call.

ADAM ROUNDED THE corner and started up the next block. The houses were old and run-down, paint peeling, shutters broken or missing, old cars and rusted toys and appliances scattered about the yards the way people in more expensive neighborhoods did with shrubbery and flower beds.

A drug deal was going down on the next corner with no regard of him, a passing truck or three boys who looked to be about eight or nine who were riding by on their bikes. A shotgun house in the middle of the block had its windows boarded up. Another had a half-rotted porch with a front door that hung askew.

According to Matilda, Quinton had rented an efficiency apartment in a house two blocks farther down Pickford Street before he'd faked his death. He'd spent even more time in Mitzi's, a neighborhood bar that was so rough that even the cops avoided it—or so Quinton used to boast to Matilda.

According to Sam, Quinton still hung out at Mitzi's and he figured Adam would find him there if he cased the joint for awhile. Adam would—if it came to that.

Adam motioned to the boys as they rode by on their bikes. Only one turned around and came back to see what he wanted. Adam pulled a twenty-dollar bill from his front jeans pocket.

"What I got to do for that?" the boy asked.

"Answer a couple of questions."

"That's all I have to do to get the twenty?"

"That's it, as long as I'm convinced you're telling the truth."

"What you want to know?"

Adam described Quinton, especially the unique patterns of his massive tattoos. "Have you seen him?"

"Once. I think he's new around here."

"When was that?"

"Two days ago. We were riding by on our bikes and he was standing on the porch of the big gray house. We slowed down to get a better look at the tattoos. He flexed his muscles and it made the eagles look like they were flying."

"What big gray house?"

"The one in the next block. On the other side of the street. Got bullet holes in the front window. A bunch of 'em. There was a drive-by a few weeks ago. Nobody got killed, though."

Adam handed the boy a twenty and reached into his pocket for another one.

The boy looked at him suspiciously. "What else you want to know?"

"Have you ever seen the man with the flying eagle tattoos with twin girls? They have red hair. They're young, not three years old yet."

"Nope. I've never seen any kids at all around that gray house."

That didn't prove the girls weren't there. Adam wouldn't have expected Quinton to parade them around the neighborhood, not when news of the abduction had gone virile.

He handed the boy the second twenty and started walking.

The big, gray house came into view as soon as he reached the corner. He stopped to assess his chances of sneaking in.

He heard footsteps but before he could turn around, something crashed into him from behind, knocking him to the pavement. His head hit the concrete and the world went blurry for a second. By the time he could see straight, feet were coming at him from every direction.

He tried to stand but the kicks were too many and too vicious. There were three guys, all big and muscular and all three enjoying themselves.

He tried to fight back, but they kicked him in his stomach, his chest, his head and even his thighs. He doubled over in pain as blood dribbled from the side of his mouth.

Before his injuries, he might have been able to hold his own with two of the men. But three guys this size against one would have been formidable odds even when he'd been in top form.

"That's enough," one of the men ordered. "Quinton said not to kill him, just to make him wish he were dead."

So Quinton was behind this. He should have known.

Finally, the kicks and the curses stopped altogether. He tried to get up but he writhed in pain and threw up on the sidewalk.

He closed his eyes and lay there, struggling for the strength to stand. The pain was excruciating, but nothing like what he'd endured in Afghanistan. Then he'd begged to die. Now he just wanted to get up and get moving again.

His daughters might be a few yards away, imprisoned by a madman.

"Did you find what you came for?"

Adam saw the shadow and looked up to see who was talking.

At least he no longer had to look for Quinton. Quinton had found him.

Chapter Twelve

"It's a tough neighborhood," Quinton said. "It's not really safe to walk around here by yourself unless you're in the members' club."

"Go to hell." Adam spit out another mouthful of blood.

"First Detective Lane, now you. I seem to be growing more popular by the hour."

"Where are Hadley's daughters?"

"Beats me. From what I hear, their mother is the most credible suspect. But you come in a close second, Adam. Can't say that I blame you if you are guilty. Who wants to put up with another man's kids?"

Adam struggled to stand. Quinton offered a hand. He ignored it.

Quinton smiled. "Since you came all the way out here, you might as well come inside, shoot the breeze, check out the closets and look under the beds."

"And have you sic your attack dogs on me again?"

Quinton pulled a pistol from his waistband. "I'll tell you what, Adam. Just to show you what a trusting guy I am, you carry the weapon. It's loaded. I'll show you the clip to prove it."

He did and then he handed the gun to Adam. "The door's unlocked. Stay as long as you like. Help yourself to a shot of whiskey to help dull the pain. But you'd best check every nook and cranny in the house while you're in there. Show up again and I'll kill you as an intruder."

Quinton turned and walked away from the house leaving Adam alone with a pistol and a body that was so bruised he could barely move.

He staggered to the house and onto the porch. He knew he wouldn't find the girls. But just maybe he'd find some sign that they'd been there. There might even be another video planted inside with directions for handling the exchange.

That was his best hope for anything good coming out of this venture into Quinton Larson's world.

Two hours later, he went back to the kitchen and poured a double shot of whiskey into a glass. He downed it in one gulp. If there was any hint that Lila and Lacy had ever been inside this house, he hadn't found it.

Yet he was more certain than ever that Quinton was behind the kidnapping. But if Quinton had realized that his chances of getting away with this were going down the toilet, he might have panicked and gotten rid of all evidence against him.

It would take a monster to kill two innocent children. Quinton fit that description to a tee.

But he wouldn't give up hope yet. Nor could he go on like this. He took out his phone and called Meghan Lambert. If she had any pull with the FBI, now was the time to use it.

They needed every advantage possible on their side.

SHELTON LANE PULLED the fax from the machine. This is what he'd been waiting for. Now he dreaded reading it. Not that he had a choice. He was a cop. Evidence had to rule.

He read it through twice, making sure he'd absorbed every detail. The facts were there. Adam Dalton was the biological father of the twins.

The girls' DNA had been easy to come by. It had been on the glass of water Hadley had taken to the kitchen during the night. Adam's had been more difficult to get. He'd had to go all the way to the hospital in Germany where Adam had gone through two years of recovery and rehab.

Too many lies usually equaled guilt.

Ironically, he'd been almost sure that Hadley was behind the disappearance from day one. Doors locked. Windows locked. Alarm not set. Ransom letter sent before the abduction. Boyfriend who shows up from out of the blue. A rich mother.

He hadn't seen Hadley as a child killer, but he had more trouble ruling out that she'd planned the kidnapping to get some of her mother's money.

And then he'd met Quinton Larson. The more the scumbag had talked, the more convinced the detective was of his guilt. But it turned out his alibi was almost airtight for the time of the abduction. He'd been caught on the security camera going in his girlfriend's apartment early evening and out the next morning at 9:22.

Lane looked up at a tapping on his door.

"Got a minute?" the police chief asked. "It's important."

"Then I've got a minute. And a fax." He handed it to the chief.

The chief read it and tossed it back to Lane's desk. "That goes right along with what I came in to discuss."

"I thought it might."

"The mayor got a call from the FBI. They're requesting that they be invited in on the case."

"And I take it he's not too keen on that," Lane said.

"No, and neither am I, not when we have as much credible evidence against Hadley O'Sullivan as we do. If they walk right in and make an arrest, we'll look like buffoons."

"I'm not completely sure Hadley is guilty," Lane said. "I can't rule out that Quinton either abducted the girls or masterminded the whole thing."

"Do you have evidence to back that up?"

"Not a shred. Just a hunch that there are still some loose ends that can't be tied up yet."

"I understand, but the pressure is on me and the department. Give it until morning. If Hadley hasn't heard from the kidnapper by then, get an arrest warrant and book her. In the meantime, I'll give you all the manpower you need to do everything possible to find those girls. Dead or alive, we need answers. For everyone's sake."

Lane couldn't argue with that.

SOMEHOW ADAM MADE it back to the ranch and spent the rest of the afternoon playing roulette ice packs. Hadley had practically gone into shock when he'd stepped through the door covered in bruises and still not standing completely straight.

She wanted to call for an ambulance, but he'd vetoed that. All he wanted was a clear path to the sofa.

After he'd downed a couple of pain pills, he explained to Hadley, R.J. and Fred how his outing had gone from bad to worse. Since then, they'd all pretty much left him to suffer in peace except for Hadley's checking on a regular basis to make sure he didn't need anything.

R.J. had presented him with steak cut from Dry Gulch beef for his left eye which was swollen almost closed earlier in the afternoon. He'd grilled four more steaks for their dinner. Hadley had baked potatoes and made a salad.

Surprisingly, Adam had eaten his fair share. His muscles were on fire, but he'd hurt worse. Much worse. Compared to the night of the ambush, today's beating seemed like a pillow fight.

He was pretty sure there were no internal injuries and no concussion. All in all, he wasn't in too bad a shape for a man who'd been treated like a soccer ball by men who could have played for any team in the North American League.

He'd retired to the family room after dinner, this time settling in the recliner. Fred joined him.

"Do you think we're just wasting your time here?" Adam asked.

"Absolutely not. The kidnapper's not going to turn his back on five million dollars. But since we haven't heard from him yet, he may need some encouragement in taking this to the next step."

"What kind of encouragement?"

"The knowledge that the police are closing in and about to make an arrest."

"Have you heard something I haven't?"

"No. But that doesn't mean that the information can't be leaked to the local media."

"I don't think they'd print something from an unnamed and unproven source."

"They'd print it if the information came from the lead detective in the case."

"And exactly how would we get Lane to agree to that?"

"You can always call and ask. It's worked for me before. Just tell him what we're trying to do. After all, it's the lives of two little girls that are on the line."

"Let's run it by Hadley first."

"Run what by me?" she said from the doorway.

Adam and Fred explained the proposal.

"Call him now," Hadley said. "If he agrees and he acts on it quickly, it might make the ten o'clock news."

Adam made the call. To all of their surprise, the detective agreed without an argument.

R.J. joined them in the family room and they talked for a while, mainly about Quinton. They were all in consensus that he was guilty as sin, but no one had a clue why he was dragging it out so long.

Hadley finally called it a night though Adam doubted she'd get much sleep. He followed soon after.

Once in his bedroom, he stripped and got under the hottest shower he could stand. He let the water sluice over his bruised, aching body.

His mind slipped back into the past, to three and a half years ago when life as he'd known it came to a painful end. He couldn't stand in a shower that night or for many nights to follow. He hadn't been able to even move his legs.

The doctors had said he might never walk again.

And he didn't need to relive that tonight. He stepped out of the shower, wrapped a towel around his waist and went back to the bedroom. He was bending over to get an undershirt from the chest when his bedroom door squeaked open.

He spun around, but one look at Hadley's face told him it hadn't been quick enough. She'd seen the scars and the burned, clotted welts of skin that deformed him.

The look of horror would give way to one of pity.

And then she'd know, but she would never understand. The deeper scars were more than skin-deep.

"Oh, Adam. Your back. What happened?"

"I was in a fight."

"No, not the bruises from today. The scars. The burns."

He yanked the shirt over his head. "Yeah, hideous, aren't they?"

"They're ghastly. The injuries must have been near fatal."

"They weren't that bad." Unless you considered misery laced with agony a bad experience.

"What happened?" she asked again.

"I took a little heat in Afghanistan, the same way a lot of guys have. That's war." His attempt at nonchalance sounded forced even to him.

"When?"

"Does it matter? The worst is over now."

"Why didn't you tell me?"

"And saddle you with a husband who might have been an invalid forever? You were young. You had everything going for you. You wanted a big family."

She closed her eyes. Tears slid from the corners and rolled down her cheeks. His heart felt as if it were breaking all over again.

Hadley stepped into the room and closed and locked the door behind her. "There was never another woman, was there?"

Chapter Thirteen

Adam didn't answer her question, but Hadley knew the answer. He'd invented the other woman to protect her from the truth. Only she'd never wanted to be protected. She'd only wanted to be loved the way she loved him.

A surge of mixed emotions tore her apart. "How could you?" she asked. "You told me you loved me. We were going to be married. How could you go through that and not tell me? How could you shut me out?"

"Hadley, this isn't the time for this conversation."

"No, the time was years ago. You left me alone and pregnant and thinking you wanted no part of me in your life. You shut me out when I needed you most. You shut me out when *you* needed me the most."

"I did what I had to do."

"Really? Just tell me how you came to the decision that our love was dispensable."

"It wasn't like that."

"Then tell me what it was like for you, Adam Dalton, because it was pure hell for me. And I didn't get the chance to do any of the deciding."

"You don't want to hear this, Hadley. Not now. Now with all you're facing."

"Stop it, Adam. Stop deciding what I do and don't

need to know. Just tell me what happened to you in Afghanistan. I deserve at least that much from you."

He turned away as if he couldn't bear to face her with the truth. "A contingent of eight marines from my platoon were on patrol when we ran into an ambush. I managed to escape and take cover. Not everyone did.

"I went back for them. I got one out without any problem. But when I went back for Charlie Pitt, an enemy shooter had moved in closer and I took three bullets to the back. One of them dangerously close to the spine."

"Charlie. Your best friend. You talked of him when we met. Were you able to save him?"

"I managed to pull him to safety, but he died minutes later from his wounds."

Always a hero and never even thinking about himself. It was one of the things she loved about him. And what she'd feared the most. In the end, it was the quality that had torn them apart.

"How did you get burned?"

"An explosive came too close while we were trying to retreat. My clothes caught on fire. One of the guys rescued me, but I don't really remember that part or anything that followed. I didn't learn until days later that only four of us survived the attack."

She'd nursed her anger toward him for years. Now all she could feel was his pain, his anguish. He was still facing away from her, so she walked over and put her arms around his waist, letting her face gingerly rest against this scarred back.

"And that's when you wrote me and told me you were involved with someone new?"

"Not immediately. I was in a coma for a few days. When I came to, I'd been moved to a hospital in Germany and was living on painkillers. I'd had one surgery but the doctors told me there were more to come and that the paralysis in my lower body might be permanent."

So he'd written her and told her there was another woman. He hadn't trusted her with the truth. She wondered if she'd had done the same if the circumstances had been reversed.

They'd had a whirlwind affair. Fireworks and excitement and dancing until dawn. Making love until her thighs had ached.

But they hadn't really known each other long enough to build unfailing trust. He hadn't stood by her the way he had since the girls had gone missing. She hadn't known the Adam she knew now. She'd never loved him the way she loved him now.

And she did love him, so very, very much.

Finally, he turned to face her and pulled her into his arms. He held her so close she could feel his heart beating aginst her own chest. When she tilted her chin and looked him in the eye, she could see love there, as well.

He kissed her, and she melted into the need and emotion. Part of her ached to stay in his arms and find comfort tonight. But nothing about that felt right. She pulled away.

"I'm sorry," Adam said.

"For the kiss?"

"For everything. Mostly for not being here for you or for the girls."

"You're here now, Adam. We'll work this out once they're safe. But right now, I can't deal with anything else."

"I understand. And I'll be here, as long as you let me stay."

Somehow she knew that this time he meant it. And she'd be here for him. True love didn't have an expiration date.

MARY NELL HAD JUST bathed the twins and put them in the pajamas she'd washed by hand and dried on the back of the headboard. They were getting used to her now and they talked more and more. They loved the puppets she'd made them out of the worn washcloths.

They were on their pallets now, eating the chicken nuggets and fries Sam had brought them.

"Let's take the girls for a ride, Sam. They're as tired of this motel room as I am."

"You'll get plenty of chance to ride once we get to Mexico City."

"I thought you said last night that we were going to Rio."

"The plans changed."

"How many more times are they going to change before we get the money?"

"None. This is a done deal."

"Does that mean you're calling Hadley tonight?"

"I'm thinking we'll call right now."

She rushed over and threw her arms around him.

"Watch it, woman. You'll spill my beer."

But she could tell he was as excited as she was.

He took out his phone. "Where is that voice disguiser?"

"I put it in the drawer next to the bed." She reached over and got it for him.

Someone tapped on the door. Mary Nell froze, the excitement dissolving so fast she grew sick.

"Take the girls into the bathroom and keep them

quiet," Sam whispered. "Don't come out or make a sound no matter what you hear."

She forced her body to move, whispering to the girls that they were playing the quiet game and must be as quiet as sleeping mice.

Lacy giggled but stopped when Mary Nell shushed her with a finger over her lips. But the loudest sound in the room was the pounding of Mary Nell's heart.

She heard the door open and then an unfamiliar voice call Sam by name. Mary Nell put her ear to the bathroom door and listened closely so that she'd hear every word.

"Quinton. What are you doing here?"

"Just stopping by to see my favorite nephew. Looks like you're not alone, though. Two little pallets on the floor. A doll. A woman's handbag. I never took you for a family man."

"How'd you find me?"

"Finding you was easy. It was figuring out that you kidnapped Hadley O'Sullivan's daughters that took some time."

Mary Nell held her breath. If Sam's uncle Quinton knew, the police were probably not far behind. In a way she'd be glad this was over. But she didn't want to go to jail.

"You're not going to turn me in, are you?"

"Turn you in?" Quinton's laugh seemed loud even behind the closed bathroom door. "I'm here to help."

"I don't need any help. I've got it all worked out. I was just about to call Hadley."

"Your plans just changed. I'm taking over. I expect a 70/30 split. The seventy goes to me, of course."

"I did all the work and took all the risks."

"Doesn't look to me like any money has crossed

hands and you're still hanging out waiting for the police to find you. Looks like you need a lot of help to me. How much ransom did you ask for?"

"Five million."

Quinton emitted a low whistle. "Boy, I like the way you think."

"I'm not a boy. I'm almost nineteen. I want fifty percent. That's more than fair and you know it."

"Spunky. I like it. Where are the girls now?"

"In the bathroom. Mary Nell, you come out now. It's only my uncle. Everything's going to be all right."

Sam opened the bathroom door.

"Want my cookie," Lacy said.

"Me, too. Me, too." Lila ran across the room to get her doll from the pallet.

"Shut those kids up," Quinton ordered. "This isn't a friggin' preschool."

Lila started to cry. Mary Nell got the cookies, sat down on one of the pallets and pulled them both onto her lap. She had a good mind to just take them and go sit in Sam's old Buick, but she wanted to hear the rest of what Quinton had to say.

"Here's the new deal," Quinton said. "First thing to remember is that the girls are dispensable. It's the money that's essential."

Dispensable. The word itself was horrifying.

"I'll talk to Hadley and make all the arrangements. We'll promise her both girls, but when we get there, we change the terms. We exchange one of the twins for the money. The other flies with us to Mexico. If we get there safely with no cops on our tail, we release the second twin in Mexico and they can come and pick her up."

Sam nodded.

Mary Nell lost control. "That's not the way we

planned this, Sam. I would have never agreed to taking one of the girls out of the country."

Quinton glared at her. "I hate to tell you this, sweetheart, but you're dispensable, too."

She was so mad she was shaking. She'd never bargained for this. And she had news for Quinton.

He was dispensable, too.

HADLEY HAD JUST fallen into a restless sleep when she was wakened by a ringing phone. She reached for her cell phone and then realized her mistake. The ringing phone was the one the kidnapper had provided.

Her pulse raced and her hands shook. She took a deep breath and picked up the phone, knowing Fred would take over after she said hello.

She pushed her hello through a lump in her throat.

"Good evening, Ms. O'Sullivan. I'm glad I caught you at home. For a second there I was beginning to wonder."

She held her breath. Fred's voice came on the line. "We were starting to wonder about you, too. But glad you called. The five million dollars is ready and waiting."

"I deal with Hadley and no one else."

"If you want the money, you deal with me, but I'm just here to simplify things. I'm not a cop or in any other kind of law enforcement. Hadley wants her daughters back. You want five million dollars. Think of me as a facilitator who only wants to protect the girls."

His words were met with silence. Panic squeezed hard on Hadley's chest until the kidnapper started talking again in the same weird voice that he'd used before.

"I'll call tomorrow night at exactly 9:00 p.m. and tell you where to meet me. When I call, I expect you be at or near the Marshall exit on I-20 between Dallas and Shreveport. I'll tell you where to go from there. But if I see any sign of a cop, Hadley will never see her girls again. Got that?"

"No cops," Fred agreed. "You were clear on that point. Now I'll share our demands. The exchange has to be in the open. No deserted houses or barns or anything where either one of us has the advantage over the other."

"Go on."

"The money in exchange for *both* girls. No tricks. Bring your friend. We know you have an accomplice. One of us will deliver the money. One of your team will deliver the girls to a point halfway between our two vehicles. We'll put the money out in the open. You'll walk the girls to it and then let them go. Then the money is yours for the taking."

"We'll check the bags for the money before the girls are released."

"I'd expect you to. There is one more thing. Before we proceed, we need to know that both girls are alive."

"I figured you would. Lacy, you and Lila come tell your mother that you're ready to come home."

Hadley heard their squeals as they raced to the phone. Her heart melted and the ache to hold them in her arms became physical pain.

"Come get me, Mommy."

"Me, too, Mommy. I love you."

Hadley could keep quiet no longer. "I love you, too, Lila. And I love you, Lacy. I'm coming to get you soon."

And then the line went dead.

HADLEY WOKE AT six the following morning after a night of short periods of restless sleep accompanied by tormenting nightmares. The twins and her running toward each other but the distance between them constantly increasing. Hundreds of twenty-dollar bills flying away in the wind while the kidnapper drove away with the girls' faces pressed to his car's windows.

Adam on fire, flames shooting into the air while his flesh melted and dripped from his bones.

She threw her legs over the side of her bed and padded to the en suite bathroom. She glanced in the bathroom mirror, almost not recognizing the haunted eyes staring back at her. She looked and felt at least ten years older than she had four days ago.

Lacy and Lila might not recognize her.

But she would recognize them and they'd know her the second she called their names and pulled them into her arms. Nothing could go wrong tonight. Fate could never be that cruel to her or her precious daughters.

Fifteen more hours and she'd hold them in her arms. Fifteen more hours and they'd meet their daddy for the first time. Fifteen more hours and she could breathe again.

She stepped out of the short cotton nightshirt and let it fall to the floor as she turned on the shower and adjusted the temperature. Then she stepped beneath the spray and let the water wash away the lingering memories from her nightmares.

Fifteen more hours and the nightmares would be behind her. She and Adam would have to work through their mistakes. It might take time, but they could do it. What they had was too precious to let it die.

The doorbell rang as she was grabbing a towel. No one ever came to her door this early, but she'd already learned that a rancher's day started at dawn.

Still, anxiety surfaced and swelled as she threw on her clothes and ran a comb through her wet hair. The smell of coffee wafted down the hallway along with the sound of voices.

Detective Lane's voice boomed above the others. A quick surge of panic sent her hurrying even faster down the long hallway.

"I have an arrest warrant."

Hadley stopped just short of the family room as the detective's words rang clear.

"I'm here to take Hadley O'Sullivan into custody."

Chapter Fourteen

Hadley stopped dead-still. The detective couldn't be serious. There had to be some mistake. Perhaps he'd misunderstood when they'd asked him to leak word of an imminent arrest.

Apprehension strained her nerves to near breaking point as she stepped into the family room and viewed the scene. Adam stood toe to toe with Lane. R.J. moseyed over to stand by Hadley as if he could protect her from the detective or the two uniformed officers at his side.

Fred had wisely stayed out of the confrontation. He had his own job to do.

"Explain the charges," Adam demanded.

"Right now it's for impeding an investigation."

Right now, suggesting it could change to something more serious in the future. "In what way have I impeded your progress?" she asked. "I've cooperated in every way I can. I have more at stake here than anyone else. It's my daughters who are missing."

"Actually, according to the information I have, it's your and Adam Dalton's daughters who are missing."

R.J. looked from Hadley to Adam. "Whoa. Run that by me again. Did you just say that those two missing little girls are my granddaughters?"

"I'm sorry, R.J.," Adam said. "I just found out yesterday myself, but we were going to tell you when this was over."

"So you'd lied to Adam as well as to me," the detective said, his gaze leveled at Hadley. "You told me the morning of the attack that you didn't know who the father was. You specifically said Adam was just a friend."

A slow burn started in Hadley's chest and then erupted into a full-blown fire. She took a step toward the detective and planted herself in front of him, hands on her hips.

"Let's set the record straight. I'm Lacy and Lila's mother. I'm a single parent, the only parent my girls have ever known. Adam is the biological father. We had an affair. He went back to Afghanistan before I even knew I'd conceived, and I never told him he was the father.

"I may not measure up to your standards for an ideal mother, but it's not cause for arrest."

"You deliberately misled an officer of the law by giving false information. We can do the rest of our talking down at central lockup."

"You wait just a goldanged minute," R.J. said. "Hadley had nothing to do with that abduction and you damn well know it. Take a look at Adam. He didn't get those bruises twiddling his thumbs and whistling Dixie. He got them out doing your job for you."

Lane pulled on his right earlobe and looked to Adam. "Care to explain what Mr. Dalton is talking about?"

"I was in Quinton Larson's neighborhood. His thugs threw me a welcoming party. Three against one. Not the best of odds."

"That's a rough neighborhood. How do you know Quinton had anything to do with the assault?"

"One of the guys on the kicking team mentioned that Quinton had said not to kill me. Guess Quinton wanted to prove what a nice guy he is. Anyway he showed up while I was still spitting up blood and offered me a tour of his house."

"His house?"

"Right. The house on Pickford Street with a window used for target practice. The DPD has surely searched it by now."

Lane ignored the comment. His nonresponse made it clear to Hadley that he hadn't been to the house on Pickford Street. Adam was proving more valuable in the investigation than she would have ever imagined.

Yet the kidnapper was still calling the shots. And she was almost positive that Quinton was behind the abduction, though he might not be in it alone.

"What kind of police department do you squirrels run in the Big D?" R.J. asked.

"I suggest you stay out of this, Mr. Dalton. I wouldn't want to take you in."

"Why not? It would make as much sense as arresting Hadley."

Lane took the handcuffs from his belt. "Hadley, give me one good reason not to arrest you."

He sounded sincere, and there was a reason, but did she dare let Lane know that they'd heard from the kidnapper? She'd told enough lies and yet the kidnapper had warned her not to involve the cops in any way.

Fred and Adam didn't really need her to rescue the girls. She wouldn't be there for them to come running into her arms, but she'd be there for the rest of their lives.

"Arrest me," she said. "Let's get it over with."

Adam came over and slipped an arm around her shoulder. "You don't have to do this, Hadley."

Lane shook his head. "Okay, I may be a bit hard-headed, but I wasn't born yesterday. It's clear that I'm not getting the straight scoop."

R.J. sneered as if this whole thing was too ridiculous to believe.

Lane turned to the two officers. "Giles, Mason. You two step outside for a minute. I need to address the suspect alone."

The two officers looked dubious, but they did as told.

"Let's start over," Lane said. "No more lies, Hadley. What do you know that I don't? Fill me in, or I swear I'll get two more warrants and arrest the whole bunch of you."

Adam put a reassuring hand to the small of Hadley's back. "I'm sorry, Hadley, but we're too close now to let this get screwed up. The kidnapper may insist on talking to you tonight. We have no choice but to trust the detective."

"It's about time," Lane said.

"We've heard from the kidnapper," Adam admitted. "R.J., would you mind getting Fred? I think he should be in on this."

Hadley swallowed hard. "Does anyone object to our moving this conference to the kitchen? I need a cup of coffee in the worst way."

An hour and two pots of coffee later, the details were ironed out to include minimal police participation, at least on the front end.

Hadley wouldn't be arrested. A sharpshooter from the SWAT team would ride in the truck with Adam and Hadley. The sharpshooter would be passed off as the negotiator that the kidnapper was already expecting.

·

He was to shoot only to save the girls' lives or after they were totally in the clear and out of the line of fire.

Lane would ride with Fred and the pilot in the Lambert's helicopter. They'd be in place nearby, ready to follow the kidnapper and arrest him after the girls were safe and before he made a successful getaway. There would also be unmarked, manned police cars in the area.

R.J. had offered to take the full five million from the bank if that was what it took to save the girls. Fred had said it wasn't necessary.

It looked good on paper. Nonetheless, Hadley was a wreck. She'd count the seconds until it was time to leave. Count and pray that she'd tuck Lacy and Lila into bed and give them a thousand good-night kisses tonight.

ONCE MARY NELL MADE up her mind what to do, she knew she had to act fast. Quinton had left with Sam last night, but he'd said he'd be back this morning as soon as he took care of a little business.

Once he was back, he'd relieve Mary Nell of her babysitting duties so that she could do whatever she needed to do on her last day in the U.S.A.

Only she didn't trust Quinton. She figured he was only trying to get rid of her. She wouldn't be surprised if he found a way to get rid of Sam, too. He didn't want half the ransom money or even seventy percent. He wanted it all.

And once he got the money, he couldn't care less if the girls lived or died. The money she and Sam were supposed to build their new life with. Money that would let her escape her stepfather who couldn't keep his hands to himself and her mother who was too hooked on drugs to care.

She threw the few items of clothing she'd bought for

the girls into a plastic grocery bag. She put the rest of the box of Cheerios and the half carton of milk into another bag. That only left the small duffel with her clothes and the few toiletries she'd brought with her when she and the girls had moved into this shabby motel.

She grabbed Lacy as the adorable toddler skipped by her. "Be still a minute and let me tie your bonnet, sweetie."

"Don't like it."

"I know but you have to wear it when we go for a ride."

"Go see Mommy."

"Right. You'll see your mommy soon."

She tied Lila's bonnet on next, pushing the escaping red curls back under the fabric of the hat. Mary Nell didn't want one strand of their red hair to show, not with everyone in the city on the lookout for two red-haired toddlers.

The TV morning news had talked of an imminent arrest of the kidnapper. Mary Nell was sick with worry that it was Sam who was about to be arrested. Then she and the girls would be left at the mercy of Quinton. She had to make sure that didn't happen.

She slung the duffel over her shoulders, hung the bags from her wrist and took both girls by the hand.

Lila balked at the door. "Need Amanda." Lila pulled free and ran back and found her beloved doll beneath the edge of her pallet.

"We're going for a ride," Mary Nell said, when Lila rejoined them. "Stay very quiet as we walk to the car. People might be sleeping."

"Get up, sleepyheads," Lacy called, ignoring the warning.

"Shhh."

Lacy looked at her sheepishly but was quiet as they walked to the back of the motel where her car was parked.

Mary Nell put the duffel and the bags in the trunk of her mother's old Chevy and then opened the back door. She hated that she didn't have their booster seats, but the risk of staying here was much greater than that of driving without the protection.

"I want you to sit very, very still while I'm driving. Keep your face away from the window and don't wave at anyone. Can you do that for me?"

"Go see Mommy," Lacy said again.

"If you do what I say."

"Pomise," Lila said.

"Good, and you have to promise, too, Lacy."

"Okay."

Mary Nell wished she could just drive them to Janice O'Sullivan's house and drop them off, but if Sam wasn't arrested, he'd be furious with her. All their plans, all their dreams of being rich and living like royalty would be gone forever.

She couldn't give up yet. But she would if it meant trusting Quinton Larson. They had to do this without him or not do it at all.

She buckled the girls into their seat belts. The fit was poor, but it was the best she could do. Then she got behind the wheel and slipped the key into the ignition. The battery groaned and died twice before it caught and the engine clattered to life.

As she drove off, she wondered if her mother had even noticed that she hadn't been home in a few nights. Hopefully, she hadn't missed her or the car.

"We're going on an adventure," she said as she turned toward the I-45 Freeway. What shall we sing?"

"Beary over the mountain."

"'The Bear Went Over the Mountain.' Great choice,

Lila. You'll have to make the motions without me because I have to steer the car."

They sang and laughed and Mary Nell told them stories—just like a normal, happy family on vacation. Not that she had ever been part of a normal, happy family.

Maybe one day if she and Sam didn't end up in jail.

She adjusted her visor and turned on the radio. She could drive forever like this, except that she couldn't afford gasoline. She had fifteen dollars left from what Sam and given her to buy food for the girls when they'd moved into the motel. She'd need that to buy more food now that they were on the run.

And she had a hundred-dollar bill she'd stolen from Quinton's wallet last night when he and Sam were out back of the motel sharing a joint.

"Go to McDonald's," Lila said when she spotted the golden arches. "Get fen fies."

"And climb and slide," Lacy added.

It was a risk, but they were all hungry and in need of a bathroom break. They stopped in Conroe, Texas, and she let the girls play for about thirty minutes. They needed the exercise.

If she stayed on I-45 south, they might have enough gas left to make it to Galveston. Galveston was on the Gulf of Mexico. It seemed the perfect place to take her stand.

Either Sam left Quinton and they did this without him, or she'd call Hadley and tell her where to find her girls.

Quinton Larson could go to hell along with her stepfather.

Quinton fumed. He should have known not to leave Sam's girlfriend here with the girls last night. Never trust a bitch with a fortune.

He paced until he saw Sam walk up to the door. He met him with a string of curses. "Your slut girlfriend took off with the kids."

"She's not a slut and she didn't take off. Mary Nell wouldn't do that to me."

"Her car's gone. She's gone. The girls are gone. If that's not taking off, what is it?"

"She must have made a run to the convenience store to get something to eat."

"She took those girls out in public. How stupid is she?"

"She is not stupid. She's just got a heart, that's all. She's not gonna let those girls go hungry."

"Get her on the phone. Order her back here on the double."

"She doesn't have a phone."

"Everybody has a phone. What is she? Homeless?"

"Her stepfather took her phone away from her last week."

"She still lives at home?"

"She's only seventeen."

"Friggin' jail bait. That figures. How come he took her phone?"

"Because he's a pervert and she doesn't like him pawing at her."

"Well, if you don't do something to get her back here before tonight, you can kiss that five million dollars that's waiting on us goodbye."

"The five millions dollars was waiting on Mary Nell and me. So stop acting like this was all your idea and we messed it up. You didn't take any of the risks. I'm the one who took the key off Mom's key ring. I stole the ether from Johnny's shop to keep the girls knocked out until I could get them out of the house. I was the one who had to clean my greasy footprints off Mrs. O'Sullivan's carpet. So don't gripe about how I've handled things when you did nothing."

"The biggest risk you took was bringing that bitch to the party. If she turns the kids over to the police, you're going to jail. Do you know what happens to kidnappers in jail?"

"I'm not going to jail."

"Then you better find those kids fast. If you don't I'm your only ticket out of here."

"Do you really think you could pull this off without having those kids to exchange for the ransom?"

"I can as long as they're still missing."

"How are you going to do that?"

"Give me time to think, and then you'll have to do exactly as I say."

Quinton started tossing around possibilities in his mind. One thing was for sure. If someone had to be sacrificed, it wouldn't be him. When the plane he'd arranged for left tonight for Mexico City, Quinton and the cash would be on it.

Janice O'Sullivan had paid for his funeral. Now she'd pay for his new life. The only thing that could be more satisfying would be getting back at Hadley O'Sullivan for trying to kill him with that damn crystal vase.

She'd thought she was too good for him, acted as if his hands were poison. She was wrong. The snobby bitch had probably never had a real man like him.

Too bad she still wouldn't get her chance to find that out. Neither Hadley nor her daughters would get any mercy from him.

THERE HAD BEEN no more phone calls from the kidnapper. Hadley took that as a good sign. As long as there were no surprises, the girls would be driving back to the ranch with them tonight.

Allowing themselves plenty of time, Hadley, Adam and the sharpshooter, Roger Orr, were in the truck and ready to go at 6:00 p.m.

Two duffel bags of twenty-dollar bills were in the backseat. Four more duffel bags were stuffed with newspaper and in the bed of the truck. Fred had decided on the extra bags at the last minute in case the plan had to be altered slightly.

Adam drove. Roger rode in the front seat with him. Hadley sat in the back with the money.

Adam and Roger talked of sports and fishing and politics, avoiding any mention of where they were going or why until they were just a few miles from their exit.

"Remember that no matter what happens, Hadley, you are not to get out of the truck," Adam warned.

"I remember." But she hadn't promised. It would be next to impossible not to jump from the truck when she saw the girls running to her.

Her contact phone rang just as they made the exit. She answered and repeated the directions as he gave them so that Adam could ask questions if he didn't understand exactly where they were to meet. This time he hadn't bothered to disguise his voice.

It wasn't familiar.

"Remind him this spot he's sending us to has to be in the open," Roger said.

He assured her that it was and then broke the connection.

"That's only about ten minutes from here," Adam said.

Hadley's heart began to pound erratically. Ten more minutes until her world swerved back into its orbit. Ten more minutes until she could hold the girls next to her heart.

Please, God, don't let anything go wrong.

The minutes dragged by until Adam pulled onto a dirt road that seemed to lead into total darkness. He switched his lights to bright.

Another mile and she spotted the car parked in the middle of the road about fifty yards in front of them. It sat at an intersection with another dirt road.

"He has his getaway planned," Hadley said.

"It won't help," Roger assured her. "If they can spot him from the helicopter, they can keep him in their sight until squad cars can pin him down."

Adam slowed and then came to a full stop in the middle of the dark, deserted road. He kept his headlights on and pointed at the other vehicle.

Adam lowered his window and picked up the bullhorn Fred had provided.

"I'll start walking toward you with two duffel bags filled with twenty-dollar bills," Adam said. "You start walking toward me with the girls. Once I see them and know they're safe, you get the rest of the money."

"I changed my mind."

Hadley's heart plunged to her stomach.

"I want to make sure that there's actually money in those bags before I deliver the girls. I pick up the bags and take them to my car and check them out. If the money's there, I'll meet you in the middle again for the rest of the money and that time I'll have the girls with me."

"Do it, Adam," she begged. "It's why we brought the extra bags with us. I don't care about the rules or even what Fred thinks is right. I just want my girls with me."

Adam went back to his bullhorn. "We accept that, but you'll get only two bags of money until we're assured the girls are safe. And no more changes. I'm bringing out the first two bags of money now." Adam reached into the backseat for the duffel bags containing R.J.'s fifty thousand dollars.

Roger readied his rifle.

Hadley stared in shock when she realized the man walking toward Adam was Matilda's son. She'd never suspected him of playing a role in the abduction. This was going to break Matilda's heart.

Quinton must have found a way to get to him.

Sam met Adam in the middle, picked up the bags and walked them back to the car. He tossed them into the front seat and then waited while the driver apparently checked out the contents of the bag.

"You've got the first installment," Adam called. "Let's see the girls."

All of a sudden the driver of the other car hit the gas and swerved into a ninety-degree spin practically running Sam down. And then the car sped away down the intersecting road, the wheels kicking up dust and gravel.

Roger pulled his rifle and pointed it at the fleeing car. He shot twice, aiming at the tires, but the car had disappeared into the darkness. Roger jumped out of the car and ordered Sam to put his hands up and not to take one step from where he was standing.

Adam radioed Fred to go after the fleeing car. Roger went over to Sam, handcuffed him and read him his rights.

It all happened in a blur for Hadley. She struggled to breathe but couldn't force oxygen into her lungs. She grew dizzy and her heart began to pound erratically.

If she couldn't get air, she was going to die. She opened the door and jumped from the truck.

Adam caught her in his arms and held her tight while she beat her fists into his chest.

"He got away. All this and he got away."

"He didn't. The helicopter will follow him. Stop fighting and hold on to me."

"But the girls..."

"We've got Sam. He'll lead us to Lacy and Lila. Detective Lane will see to that."

They were words, only words, but she was no longer fighting for breath. The vertigo lessened. The world stopped bucking.

"I'll be here for you, Hadley," Adam whispered. "I promise I'll be here for you. But I need you to be here for me."

The pleading in his voice finally got through to her. She wasn't the only one who was afraid. She wasn't the only who was hurting.

Adam rocked her in his arms until she could stand by herself. But he couldn't still the fear that was driving her out of her mind.

The fear that she might never see Lacy and Lila again.

MARY NELL WOKE TO bright sunlight streaming through the window of her motel room. The room was no bigger than the one she'd shared with the girls in Dallas, but it was clean. And instead of a noisy highway outside her window, there was the Gulf of Mexico.

She stretched and then eased out of bed so as not to wake the girls. They'd slept with her last night instead of on the floor. She'd never expected to grow so fond of them. She hoped she and Sam had lots of kids.

The time for them to turn Lacy and Lila over to Hadley had come and gone. Hopefully, Quinton had given up and gone, as well. Then she and Sam could make this work.

He'd be upset with her for running out on him, but once she explained that she'd done it for them and for the girls, he'd understand.

Unless he'd been arrested. No. She had to stay positive. Sam was at home in his bed, just waking up and wondering where she was and why she hadn't gotten in touch with him.

There was a phone in the room but she was nervous about making the call in case Sam was with Quinton. But she had no choice. She got an outside line and called his number. There was no answer. She left a brief message asking Sam to come and get them in Galveston. She couldn't bear going back to that sleazy motel where they'd been staying.

After that, she stood at the window and admired the view. There were sailboats in the distance and a sandy playground just across the street from the motel and right on the beach.

Too bad she didn't dare take the girls there. She was afraid to even take them to the breakfast room for the free food. She should go now while they were still asleep and bring something back for them to eat.

And then they'd wait on Sam to come for them. He loved her. He wouldn't let her down.

She slipped into a pair of white shorts and a tank top and ran her fingers through her hair. Then she stepped into her flip-flops, locked the girls in the room and went to find food.

She returned with a tray loaded with yogurt, cereal, fruit and juice for the girls and with a bagel, cream cheese and coffee for herself. The girls were still sound asleep.

She turned the TV on low to see if there was any more talk of an arrest being made.

She didn't have to wait long before her fears turned to shock. She blinked, unable to believe that was Sam's image on the screen. He was in handcuffs and walking next to Detective Lane. She grabbed the remote to turn up the volume.

Sam had been arrested in an attempt to collect a ransom. Quinton had gotten away with fifty thousand dollars. There was no mention of her but Sam had given them Quinton's name as an accomplice.

Quinton who was walking around a free man. Hopefully, he'd left the country with the fifty thousand, but what if he hadn't? He knew she had the girls. He'd track her down. He'd take them from her and then demand the rest of the five million from Hadley.

But he wouldn't let it go at that. He'd find a way to get even with her.

She had to do something and do it quick.

Before Quinton came banging on the door.

SAM'S CELL PHONE VIBRATED. Quinton picked it up and saw that there was a missed call and a waiting message. The phone must have rung while he was in the bathroom. He called voice mail and listened to the message.

"We're at the SunFun Motel in Galveston. Come for us."

I'm on my way, Mary Nell. I'm on my way.

Chapter Fifteen

Hadley sat in the porch swing, a cup of coffee that had grown cold clutched in her hand. She stared straight in front of her but didn't really see anything.

Her brain was numb, the rest of her body an aching mass of muscles that seemed disconnected and unresponsive.

The detective, Adam, Fred, and even R.J. had tried to convince her that progress had been made. Either they thought she was a fool or they were fooling themselves.

Even though the helicopter was in the air in minutes after the getaway car had speeded from sight, the car had never been spotted again. Hundreds of police and private citizens were combing that area now looking for the car and the girls. R.J. and all three of the Lambert brothers were among that group.

Detective Lane had insisted that she, Adam and Fred stay at the ranch in case Quinton tried to get in touch with them. She had little hope that would happen. Quinton was most likely across the border by now with R.J.'s fifty thousand dollars.

No one had an explanation for why he hadn't gone through with the planned ransom exchange except that he must have suspected a trap.

If Sam knew where Lacy and Lila were, he wasn't

admitting it. According to Lane, even under intense interrogation, Sam had stuck to his original story. He'd said that Quinton had come to him yesterday and threatened Alana if he didn't cooperate with him.

Lacy and Lila could be locked in a dark closet somewhere, starving and crying for their mother to come and save them. They might be outside, wandering in a patch of woods along any highway, lost and afraid. They could be…

No. She couldn't bring herself to even think the dreaded word.

Nausea hit again and she grew so dizzy the cup slipped from her fingers and broke into dozens of pieces. The coffee sloshed on her legs and feet. She didn't bother to wipe it off.

Her phone jingled announcing a new text. She checked the caller ID. The sender information had been blocked.

In spite of her crippling depression, she felt a twinge of hope as she opened the message.

If you want to get your daughters back, meet me ASAP in Galveston. I'm not the kidnapper, but I know where they are. More info to follow.

Hadley knew the odds were that this was a hoax. She warned herself not to get her hopes up again. And yet traitorous anticipation laced her heart.

She jumped from the swing and ran to find Adam. This time she didn't want police involvement or a negotiator. This time she only wanted Adam with her. She'd take no chance in scaring off anyone who might know the whereabouts of her Lacy and Lila.

ADAM CALLED AND MADE the arrangements with Durk Lambert. They would have to drive into Dallas to board the plane, but the flight to Galveston on the company jet would get them there about two hours faster than driving.

Adam strongly suspected the call was a ruse and that the trip was a wild-goose chase, but he agreed readily to make the trip with her. Any chance was better than none.

They touched down at a small private airport in Galveston at 11:06. The rental car Adam had ordered ahead of time was waiting. There had been no more texts.

The pilot stood at the door as they started to descend the narrow steps to the tarmac. "Do you have any idea what time you'll want to fly back to Dallas?"

"I'm hoping we won't need more than an hour at the most," Adam said, "but I can't guarantee this won't take longer."

"Take all the time you need." He took a card from his pocket and handed it to Adam. "Give me about a thirty-minute heads-up if you can. I'll be in the area."

"Thanks, "Adam said.

They hadn't told the pilot the nature of their business. Nor had Durk, but Hadley was certain he could tell from their demeanor that this was not your normal business trip.

Adam took care of the paperwork on the rental. There was still no follow-up to the earlier text. He opened the car door for her. "No use to just hang around the airport. We may as well find a coffee shop on the beach."

They had just taken their first sip of coffee when the text came through. Hadley picked up the phone but said a silent prayer before she checked the message. She read it silently to herself and then read it out loud.

"The SunFun Motel. Room 217. I'm sorry."

Frustration took hold again. "I'm sorry. That can mean anything. Sorry the texter had changed his or her mind about talking to me? Sorry he got our hopes up for nothing. Sorry that..."

"Find the hotel on your phone's GPS," Adam said, calm in the face of immense frustration—as usual. Calm but not immune. His fingers had tightened on the wheel and his muscles bunched and flexed beneath his light blue sport shirt.

"It's 6.2 miles away," Hadley said. She gave him directions and cursed every red light.

"I can't stand this. I'm calling the motel," she said. "I'll ask for Room 217 and see if someone answers."

She made the call. "Room 217, please."

"I'm sorry. The guest in that room checked out just a few minutes ago."

Hadley mouthed the words *checked out* for Adam. He grimaced.

"Please ring the room anyway," Hadley said.

"I'm pretty sure I saw her drive away, but I'll ring the room."

"Thanks."

Hadley checked the GPS while the phone rang. "Turn right in six hundred feet."

She was about to hang up when the phone clicked and she heard a noise as if it had been dropped. "Hello, she called into the phone. Hello. Is anyone there?"

"It's Mommy."

The familiar voice wrapped tight around her heart. Her throat closed. Tears burned at the corners of her eyelids.

"Lacy, is that you?"

"Come get me, Mommy."

"I'm coming, sweetheart. I'm coming. Is Lila with you?"

"Yes. She being bad. She took my cookie."

"We'll buy more cookies. We'll buy all the cookies you want."

Adam took her hand and squeezed it as he jerked to a stop in front of Room 217 at the SunFun Motel. "Ask her who's with her."

Dread choked Hadley's joy. She'd been so excited at the sound of her daughter's voice that she'd never considered that this might be a trap. If Quinton was in that room with them, if this was another of his schemes.

He'd never let them just walk in and walk away with the girls.

"Who's in the room with you, sweetheart?"

"Lila?"

"Who else?"

"Amanda. Mary Nell left us."

Adam was already out of his truck when the door to Room 217 opened and Lila stepped onto the outdoor walkway. Adam flew up the steps and grabbed her. She started to scream and he quickly set her back down.

Lacy ran out of the room and started kicking him.

With tears streaming down her face, Hadley raced to his rescue. She fell to her knees and both girls tumbled into her arms.

"Don't cry, Mommy."

But she couldn't stop crying and laughing and kissing.

"This is Adam," she said when the girls had endured all the slobbering attention they could stand. "He's my friend."

She'd tell them he was their father later when they'd had time to get to know him. They'd soon love him the way she did. The way she'd always loved him. The way she always would, even though they still had a few serious barriers to hurdle.

Adam picked up both girls and started toward the steps. Hadley took one quick look inside the motel room. She didn't see another soul, but there was food scattered about the room. At least her babies had not starved.

"Wanna go home, Mommy," Lila said when she caught up with them.

"Me, too, sweetheart. Me, too."

Oddly, when she's said home, she was actually thinking of the Dry Gulch Ranch.

QUINTON SWERVED INTO the left lane and passed an 18-wheeler that was going five miles over the speed limit. He cursed the traffic the way he had ever since leaving Dallas.

By now, the stupid broad would have surely heard that Sam had been arrested. There was no telling what she was planning.

Most likely she'd try to get the ransom for herself and end up in jail with Sam. He had to get to her before she screwed up everything.

He needed the girls and then he'd collect the rest of his five million. But one stupid move by Hadley and the next time she saw her daughters, they'd be dead.

UNABLE TO BE MORE than a few inches away from the girls, Hadley had sandwiched herself between them in the backseat of the car. The girls were giggly and full of chatter as they drove to the airport.

They were not only unhurt, there were no apparent signs that they'd been frightened during the kidnapping ordeal. That did not sound as if they'd been left at the mercy of Quinton.

Lacy had mentioned the name Mary Nell. Perhaps she'd been the one who'd cared for them and kept them safe.

Hadley leaned forward and touched Adam on the shoulder. "I should have gone inside the hotel room and looked around. There might have been a note from whoever texted me."

"If there is, the cops will find it. I think we should call the detective now and let him take care of the case from here on out."

"And I have to call Mother and R.J. I should do that now." She took out her phone and made the calls. Her mother was so ecstatic she didn't even complain about Adam. She'd talked to both of the girls, though. And then she'd started singing "Amazing Grace" right over the phone.

R.J. was silent for at least a minute. When he finally said something, it was a mumbled old Texas saying that had little relevance to the situation. But she'd swear he was crying.

"I don't think your father is used to showing emotion," she said when she and Adam had both finished their calls.

"I have no idea what R.J. is about or what affects him. But he came through for us when we needed his help. He opened his home and his pocketbook with no strings attached."

"I think he's trying hard to connect with you, Adam."

"Maybe he should have practiced back when I was the age Lacy and Lila are now."

"Everyone makes mistakes, Adam. Look at the years

we lost together because of ours. What did Lane say?" she asked, changing the subject.

The scars in R.J. and Adam's relationship would not fade overnight any more than the scars on Adam's back would. But given a chance, they could at some time in the future.

"The detective admitted he owed you an apology," Adam said. "He said he'll deliver it in person when we get back to Dallas and promised that he'll track down and arrest Quinton no matter how long it takes."

Adam pulled into the almost empty airport parking lot. Traveling by private jet was far less complicated than taking a commercial airline.

Lila tugged on her arm. "Where my Amanda?"

The doll. They'd forgotten the doll. "Did you have her in the motel?"

"She's in the covers." Lila began to cry.

"We can't leave Amanda in the covers," Adam said. "We'll go right back and get her."

Lila quit crying. Adam turned the car around and exited the parking lot.

"When we get to the SunFun, I'll run in and get the manager to let me back into the room to get it," Hadley said. Hopefully the room hadn't been cleaned and serviced yet. She wanted a chance to look around, though she had no idea what she was looking for other than the doll.

"Room 217 hasn't been cleaned, but I'm afraid I can't let you in there."

"I only need to pick up my daughter's doll. I can't go back to Dallas without it. She'll cry all the way and she won't go to sleep tonight without it."

"I sympathize, believe me, I do. But we have orders

from the police to let no one into that room until they give us the all-clear. They didn't say why."

"Give me a minute." Hadley made a quick call to Detective Lane. He owed her more than an apology. She was ready to collect on the debt.

Within five minutes, the local police called and gave the manager permission to let Hadley into the room with orders that she was only to get the doll and leave.

The manager took her to the room and unlocked the door. "You're on your own. I normally follow police orders exactly, but I'm not getting in the middle of this. You do what you have to."

"Thank you."

Hadley quickly found the doll, hidden in the bed covers, just as Lila had said. She picked it up and hugged it to her chest as she scanned the rest of the room.

Two old-fashioned bonnets lay atop the room's small desk. The motel notepad that rested beside them held a meticulously printed note.

I'm sorry for my part in the abduction. I took care of your girls as best I could. They are precious. Take care of them and give them lots of love. And make sure Quinton Larson never comes near them again. He is an evil man.

Ignoring the detective's orders, she tore the note from the pad and stuck it into her pocket.

"Well, well, if it isn't little Miss Goody Two-shoes. What luck to run into you here."

She spun around just as Quinton Larson turned the safety latch on the door.

Chapter Sixteen

Hadley backed away from Quinton, trying to think beyond the sudden crippling fear. "If you come any closer, I'll scream."

He reached down and pulled a long, sharp knife from a scabbard hidden inside his right boot. "Go ahead. See how much scream you can get out before I slice your jugular."

"What do you want from me?"

"The rest of the five million you owe me."

"The ransom only stood if you produced the girls. You didn't."

"No, but now I have you. A new kidnapping. A new deal. Five million seems such a paltry sum for a full-grown woman."

"You can't get away with this, Quinton. The police are on their way here right now. They'll break through that door and shoot you."

He smirked and shook his head. "That's not the way it works, Hadley. You should know that. Didn't you learn anything from the professional negotiator you hired? The one in control sets the terms. Your boyfriend will meet them if he wants you back alive."

And she wanted to be alive. Her life was starting anew. She had Adam and Lacy and Lila. She had everything she'd ever dreamed of. She couldn't lose it to a monster.

"What is it you want, Quinton?"

He placed the blade of the knife along her cheek. "Get your boyfriend on the line. I'll do the talking. While I do, why don't you slip into something comfortable? We can start celebrating where we left off on your fourteenth birthday."

Dread crawled over her flesh. She couldn't bear to think of him touching her private places and defiling her in ways that would never leave her mind.

He trailed the tip of the knife along her skin until it reached a spot just below her earlobe. "Make the call or Adam Dalton will find you drowning in your own blood."

He was going to kill her no matter what she did. He'd been waiting to get back at her for fifteen years. For him, this wasn't only the money, it was payback time. And if Adam rushed to her rescue, he'd kill him as well.

Lila and Lacy wouldn't have either parent to look after them. She loved them and Adam too much to let that happen.

She took the phone from her pocket and punched in the private number of Detective Shelton Lane.

ADAM EXPLODED BEFORE Lane had finished the first sentence.

"I'll kill him."

"Don't go off half-cocked, Adam. I've talked to the local authorities. They're sending officers to monitor the situation until a SWAT team arrives. Let them handle this. They're skilled in dealing with dangerous situations."

What the hell did the detective think the marines were? Boy Scouts?

Quinton was a madman. He couldn't be trusted to let Hadley live until he could get to her, much less until a SWAT team would arrive from who knew where. Especially after she'd already double-crossed him with that call to the detective.

Adam grabbed both girls and raced toward the outdoor stairwell. He ducked into the room where the cleaning woman was emptying trash cans.

"I need your keys. And I need you to take the girls down to the office and stay with them until the cops arrive. They're on their way."

She started to protest, but must have decided he was too frantic to argue with. She pushed the keys into his hand.

"Go downstairs with this nice lady. Your mommy loves you and she'll be right back," he whispered when both girls began to whine.

He had a key. He had no weapon. He grabbed a steak knife from an empty room service plate. What he wouldn't give for a government-issued AK-47 now.

Adam slid the key into the lock of 217 as the cleaning woman led the girls downstairs. He turned the key and burst into the room.

One look and he knew he hadn't been fast enough.

Chapter Seventeen

Hadley was lying on the floor, faceup, terror imprinted in the lines of her face. Her blouse was ripped and she was naked from the waist down. Quinton was on top of her, his unzipped trousers hanging below his hips.

"Get out, Adam," Hadley begged. "Please, just go away. Quinton has a knife and a gun."

Adam saw the blade of the knife then. The handle was hidden in the loose folds of Hadley's ripped blouse. The point of the blade was pressed again her jugular vein. One jab of the blade and she'd bleed to death in minutes.

"Close the door behind you, Adam. Sit down and watch. I'll show you how a real man takes care of a woman."

Adam fought to stay calm. Blunt force was no match for a knife at the throat. "A real man doesn't have to hold his woman at knifepoint. They flock to us."

"Yeah. Adam Dalton. Big hero. What good are those medals now?"

"I thought this was all about money, Quinton. Do you want the rest of that five million or not?"

"Did you come to deliver it?"

"That's what we're here for. We got a text that said bring money, take home girls."

Adam had his interest now, but the knife was still at Hadley's throat. "Let Hadley walk. Hold me prisoner instead and I'll have R.J. cart in the money."

"You'll have to do better than that, Adam. How about show me the money first."

Fortunately, Adam had learned a thing or two from Fred Casey and he could see the greed burning in Quinton's eyes.

"Doesn't work that way," Adam said. "The man with the gold makes the rules. Hadley walks or...."

"Or I slice her pretty little throat," Quinton said.

"And then you go to jail a poor man. But you better decide which it's to be quickly. If R.J. doesn't hear from me in..." Adam checked his watch. "Not looking good. Three minutes before R.J. calls the cops."

The knife slowly slid from Hadley's throat. Quinton still held it and he was still in stabbing distance. But Quinton was off balance and struggling with his trousers now and Adam's bluff wouldn't hold forever.

Adam lunged at Quinton and took him down. They wrestled for the knife. And then a crashing blow sent shattered glass falling like rain.

Quinton's eyes rolled back in his head and his body went limp.

"It's the old slam him with the heavy glass trick," Hadley said. "I didn't see a vase but the lamp worked even better."

"Remind me to never make you mad."

But she was shaking as she yanked her blouse together as best as she could and then quickly redressed the rest of the way.

Adam pulled her into his arms. "Did he hurt you? Did he..."

"No, but he would have if you hadn't come to the rescue."

"You helped with that."

"And that's how it should be, Adam. We're in this together. Couples have to share the bad with the good."

"I love you, Hadley O'Sullivan. I love you with all my heart, but…"

She shushed him with a kiss that set his soul on fire. And for the first time since his injuries, he felt a sensual stirring below his belt.

That had to be a very good sign.

Quinton began to stir. A second later, a gaggle of cops rushed into the room, guns in hand.

"You're Hadley O'Sullivan," one of them said.

"I am. And the monster on the floor is Quinton Larson. He's all yours."

Adam slipped an arm around her waist and led her toward the door.

One of the cops blocked their path. "Where do you think you're going?"

"To get my daughters," they answered in unison.

That was also the way it was meant to be.

Epilogue

Three months later

R.J. stumbled backward as he lifted the toolbox to toss it into the back of Adam's truck. Adam rushed over to steady him.

"You, okay?"

"Yeah. Doctor said to expect these dizzy spells to hit now and again."

And they'd hit more often as the days went by. But R.J. was hanging in there. He was a tough old buzzard. Adam still couldn't make himself call him dad, but they were making progress in their relationship and he figured that would come one day soon.

R.J. leaned against the back of the truck. "Any news on Quinton's status?"

"The judge denied bail so it looks as if he'll be in jail until the trial."

"Even that's too good for him," R.J. said. "What about the rest of Matilda's family?"

"Sam's out on bail, but I suspect he'll do some jail time, as he should. According to Janice O'Sullivan, Matilda and her daughter are getting some counseling that Janice both encouraged and insisted on paying for."

"Good for Janice."

"Yep. She can be forgiving when she wants to. Hadley says Matilda and her daughter are working hard on going on with their lives as best they can. Matilda's upset about her son, as any mother would be, but he's cooperating with the prosecutor now, so he may get some leniency."

"And how is Janice?"

"Doing great. Still not thrilled about having me back in the family, but the oncologist feels confident that the cancer was completely removed."

"What about Mary Nell? She saved my granddaughters' lives. I'd hate to see her spend time in prison."

"Lane says she's likely to get off with an extended parole. She not only saved their lives, she made what could have been a horrible ordeal for them into a positive experience. They still ask about her."

"I'm thinking I'll offer her a college scholarship, I mean, if that's all right with you and Hadley. Apparently she was a good student, and she needs to get of that house with her mother and stepfather."

"That's fine with me," Adam said, "and I'm sure it will be great with Hadley. And speaking of Hadley, I'd best get back to work on the house. Do you want to drive out to the site with me?"

"Not this time. But, Adam, in case I haven't said this before. I'm damn pleased you, Hadley and my granddaughters are moving onto the ranch."

"So am I, R.J. So am I."

"OKAY, COWBOY. I know R.J. put you in charge of making improvements to the ranch, but the house is my department."

"You drive a hard bargain, Mrs. Dalton."

"And I carry a big vase, Mr. Dalton."

"So what changes do you want in the plans now?"

"More bedrooms."

"More than five?"

"We already have two children. I'd like to have at least three more. And we need guest rooms."

"Can we put the one for your mother under a separate roof?"

"Absolutely not. She's coming around. She hasn't reminded me how you broke my heart in at least…."

"Two days," Adam said, finishing her sentence. "But I'm just teasing. I kind of like the way she reminds me of how lucky I am to have you."

"We are lucky, Adam. We have our precious daughters. So as to my list of things that make my world perfect. You look dynamite in jeans and boots. And we are building a house on this beautiful ranch. What more could we want?"

"Nothing, Hadley. Absolutely nothing—except for a couple of sons."

He pulled her into his arms and into the thrill of his kiss. She would never grow tired of kissing Adam.

He nibbled an earlobe. "You know, since the girls are napping, we could go inside and work on those sons right now."

One more thing to be thankful for—not that she wouldn't have loved him in any condition.

But Adam Dalton was all man.

* * * * *

REQUEST YOUR FREE BOOKS!
2 FREE NOVELS PLUS 2 FREE GIFTS!

⊕HARLEQUIN®

INTRIGUE®

BREATHTAKING ROMANTIC SUSPENSE

YES! Please send me 2 FREE Harlequin Intrigue® novels and my 2 FREE gifts (gifts are worth about $10). After receiving them, if I don't wish to receive any more books, I can return the shipping statement marked "cancel." If I don't cancel, I will receive 6 brand-new novels every month and be billed just $4.74 per book in the U.S. or $5.24 per book in Canada. That's a savings of at least 14% off the cover price! It's quite a bargain! Shipping and handling is just 50¢ per book in the U.S. and 75¢ per book in Canada.* I understand that accepting the 2 free books and gifts places me under no obligation to buy anything. I can always return a shipment and cancel at any time. Even if I never buy another book, the two free books and gifts are mine to keep forever.

182/382 HDN F42N

Name	(PLEASE PRINT)	
Address		Apt. #
City	State/Prov.	Zip/Postal Code

Signature (if under 18, a parent or guardian must sign)

Mail to the Harlequin® Reader Service:
IN U.S.A.: P.O. Box 1867, Buffalo, NY 14240-1867
IN CANADA: P.O. Box 609, Fort Erie, Ontario L2A 5X3

**Are you a subscriber to Harlequin Intrigue books
and want to receive the larger-print edition?
Call 1-800-873-8635 or visit www.ReaderService.com.**

* Terms and prices subject to change without notice. Prices do not include applicable taxes. Sales tax applicable in N.Y. Canadian residents will be charged applicable taxes. Offer not valid in Quebec. This offer is limited to one order per household. Not valid for current subscribers to Harlequin Intrigue books. All orders subject to credit approval. Credit or debit balances in a customer's account(s) may be offset by any other outstanding balance owed by or to the customer. Please allow 4 to 6 weeks for delivery. Offer available while quantities last.

Your Privacy—The Harlequin® Reader Service is committed to protecting your privacy. Our Privacy Policy is available online at www.ReaderService.com or upon request from the Harlequin Reader Service.

We make a portion of our mailing list available to reputable third parties that offer products we believe may interest you. If you prefer that we not exchange your name with third parties, or if you wish to clarify or modify your communication preferences, please visit us at www.ReaderService.com/consumerchoice or write to us at Harlequin Reader Service Preference Service, P.O. Box 9062, Buffalo, NY 14269. Include your complete name and address.

HI13R

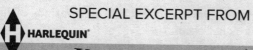
*When mysterious threats are made on the lives of
Kate Langsdon and her young daughter, only decorated
former Austin police officer Ben Harding is willing to
protect them at any cost.*

The warmth of his hands on her arms sent shivers throughout her body. "Really, it's fine," she said, even as she let him maneuver her to sit on the arm of the couch.

Ben squatted, pulled the tennis shoe off her foot and removed her sock. "I had training as a first responder on the Austin police force. Let me be the judge."

Kate held her breath as he lifted her foot and turned it to inspect the ankle, his fingers grazing over her skin.

"See? Just bumped it. It'll be fine in a minute." She cursed inwardly at her breathlessness. A man's hands on her ankle shouldn't send her into a tailspin. Ben Harding was a trained professional—touching a woman's ankle meant nothing other than a concern for health and safety. Nothing more.

Then why was she breathing like a teenager on her first date? Kate bent to slide her foot back into her shoe, biting hard on her lip to keep from crying out at the pain. When she turned toward him she could feel the warmth of his breath fan across her cheek.

"You should put a little ice on that," he said, his tone as smooth as warm syrup.

Ice was exactly what she needed. To chill her natural reaction to a handsome man, paid to help and protect her, not touch, hold or kiss her.

Kate jumped up and moved away from Ben and his gentle fingers. "I should get back outside. No telling what Lily is up to."

Ben caught her arm as she passed him. "You felt it, too, didn't you?"

Kate fought the urge to lean into him and sniff the musky scent of male. Four years was a long time to go without a man. "I don't know what you're talking about."

Ben held her arm a moment longer, then let go. "You're right. We should check on Lily."

Kate hurried for the door. Just as she crossed the threshold into the south Texas sunshine, a frightened scream made her racing heart stop.

Don't miss the dramatic conclusion to
TRIGGERED by Elle James.

Available July 2013, only from Harlequin Intrigue.

HARLEQUIN®

INTRIGUE®

IN MAVERICK COUNTY,
HE WAS THE LAW.

When Caitlyn Barnes unexpectedly shows up at his ranch,
Texas marshal Harlan McKinney has no idea his ex-lover
is trailing a heaping pile of danger. And soon Caitlyn and
Harlan are on the run out of Maverick County. Tracked by
a killer who's always one step ahead, Harlan is blindsided
by an explosive secret from the past—and a passion that's
even more dangerous....

OUTLAW LAWMAN

BY *USA TODAY* BESTSELLING AUTHOR
DELORES FOSSEN

Available June 18 wherever books are sold.
Only from Harlequin® Intrigue®.